THE ARCHERS
TO THE VICTOR THE SPOILS

D0806779

THE ARCHERS

TO THE VICTOR THE SPOILS

Jock Gallagher

BBC BOOKS

Other titles in
the Archers series

RETURN TO AMBRIDGE
BORCHESTER ECHOES

Published by BBC Books
A division of BBC Enterprises Ltd
Woodlands, 80 Wood Lane, London W12 OTT

First published 1988
© Jock Gallagher 1988

ISBN 0 563 20599 7

Set in 10/11 Times Roman by Opus, Oxford
and printed in Great Britain by
Richard Clay Ltd, Bungay, Suffolk

CHAPTER ONE

The sun shone through the open window at Brookfield Farm and Phoebe Archer hummed carelessly to herself as she washed the red clay off her hands. She smiled at the cheerful birdsong and watched with idle fascination as the rivulets of water from the pump attacked the grime.

It was still only eight o'clock but she had been up for more than a couple of hours already .. . . . not that she minded, especially on a beautiful summer morning like this, when the clean country air wafted through the house in a gentle breeze.

Earlier, she had helped to milk the cows and then she'd collected the eggs from the hen-coops. Now she had just finished bringing in fresh vegetables for the mid-day family meal, which had to be on the table by noon. A hand-picked selection of carrots, parsnips and swedes lay in the sink waiting to be scraped. That would be her next job.

Phoebe Archer was born to be a farmer's wife and she enjoyed the hard work that went with it. She had married a good man – John Archer was the best in Ambridge, she believed – and had cheerfully become his unpaid labourer and helpmate when he was lucky enough to get the tenancy of the hundred-acre farm twenty years earlier when he was only twenty-five. She had been very proud the day they had moved into the big, oak-beamed farmhouse.

For years they had tended the stock and tilled the rich Borsetshire soil on their own. In those early days, cheap as labour was, they couldn't afford to take on any other help. That meant working all the hours that God sent . . . and a few they kept up their sleeves for emergencies! Many was the day they had tumbled into bed after twelve hours in the fields, too exhausted to even speak to each other.

Now it was getting easier all the time and it wouldn't be long before young Daniel and Ben were back from the war and could join their father on the farm. Then she wouldn't know what to do with all her spare time, Phoebe thought.

The water on her hands was icy cold but that wasn't what sent a shiver down her spine. It was the sudden reminder of the war. It was nearly two years since young Daniel had proudly announced that he had taken the King's Shilling and joined the Borsetshire Regiment. She could still remember vividly the shock and despair she had felt when she learnt that he was going off to fight the Germans.

Of course, she knew it was his duty, and she also knew that she should be pleased and proud that he had grown into such a fine young man that he hadn't given a thought for his own safety. Out loud, she had said all the right things. She had told everyone she was pleased and proud because that's what everyone expected to hear . . . but later that night, she had quietly cried herself to sleep.

How she had managed to prevent herself crying in public when the time came for him to leave, she would never know. It had taken all her willpower to hold back the tears for fear of embarrassing her son.

All the anguish had been repeated twelve months later when Ben reached his nineteenth birthday and did exactly the same thing. Both lads were now on active service . . . somewhere in France, she presumed, but she hadn't heard from either of them in months and couldn't be sure of anything. The last thing she'd had was one of those awful printed field-postcards from Ben, with a tick against the line that said: "I am quite well." The cards were probably for poor lads who couldn't write. Phoebe couldn't understand why her Ben, who was perfectly capable of doing so, hadn't written a letter.

The sharp crack of a flare pistol somewhere over to the left was followed by a brilliant light tearing a great hole in the black night sky. Another crack, and away to the

6

right a second very light shot into the air and hung there, exposing the most forward position of the British troops defending the Ypres Salient, in what some people called the Great War.

Stranded in the narrow stretch of no-man's-land between the lines, young Ben Archer grovelled deeper into the stinking mud and prayed that the enemy wouldn't be able to see him among the grim debris of the war.

Forever, it seemed, he had suffered gut-wrenching pangs of hunger and cold and tiredness and pain. From the moment he and the battalion had first set foot in this god-forsaken spot – was it France or Belgium? – the reality of war had hit him. He knew it was still high summer, but this was like no summer he had ever experienced. No birds sang in this summer, and the landscape had been swept clean of its lushness. Trees and bushes and every blade of grass had disappeared. Even when the sun did shine, it was upon a scene of numbing desolation.

Back home in Ambridge – was it really only a year ago? – he had accepted the picture of brave lads fighting for their King and country. Fancying himself in khaki, he hadn't hesitated to follow his elder brother Daniel into the Colours – a posting to the Front with the Borsetshire Regiment had then represented the opportunity for heroism, a chance to show the Germans that nothing could subdue the courage of the fighting Tommy.

Now, in this hell-hole of waste that the officers called the Ypres Salient and said must be held at all costs, Ben Archer no longer felt hunger or cold, tiredness or pain. He felt nothing but blind fear.

With mud in his mouth and his nostrils, he crawled frantically towards the only cover there was – the body of a dead comrade. The single pip on a torn epaulette identified the corpse – newly-dead, Ben could tell, because blood was still seeping from a terrible chest wound – as a young officer. Ben had little concern for which of them it was and even less shame about hiding behind the dead man.

Heavy machine-gun fire raked the battlefield. Ben felt himself convulse in panic as bullets thudded into the body. He pressed himself even harder into the mud. To his horror the lifeless hulk – partially-lifted by the force of the shells – twisted around and then slumped over on top of him. He lay there staring dumbly into two wide-open but unseeing eyes only inches away.

A scream formed somewhere deep inside him but was immediately strangled by the greater strength of self-preservation. Any noise from him would attract another salvo of bullets.

There was nothing he could do to end the nightmare. To push away the dead officer would be to leave himself exposed to the flesh-tearing heavy shells and almost certain death. But how long could he lie there in this macabre embrace? Would his own death, after all, be preferable? Wasn't that the only way the war could end for him anyway?

Just as suddenly as they had changed night into day, the flares disappeared and darkness returned to the stark battlefield. With it came an eerie silence. Ben couldn't be sure what held the greatest terror for him, the crashing noise of gun fire or this deathly stillness. One day, he vowed, he would be heroic . . . but not this time. This time he would be satisfied to live to fight the hero's war another day.

Now came the agony of wondering if he was the only one left alive on his side. With the moon hidden by heavy rainclouds, he couldn't see anything . . . nor could he hear anything. Had everyone been killed?

Almost immediately, he knew that they hadn't.

"Ben!"

His name was whispered from somewhere up in front of him.

"Can you help me? I've been hit."

At first he didn't recognise the hoarse voice. Was it a German trick to lure him out of his hiding place?

"Ben, for God's sake help me. Please . . . can you hear me? Are you all right?"

The accent was unmistakably from Borsetshire. Ben remembered that another Ambridge lad, Percy Hood, had been in the position just ahead of him.

"Is that you, Percy?"

He asked the question so quietly that he wondered if the words ever left his lips.

"Aye, it is . . . what's left of me. Help me. Please help me."

The agony in the voice roused Ben from his self-pity. Gently he pushed aside the dead officer. As the moon appeared fleetingly from behind the clouds he saw that he had been sheltering behind the body of Cedric Lawson-Hope, the son of the village squire whose paternalistic mantle enveloped the whole of Ambridge.

Blindly he groped around for his rifle although he didn't know why. It was almost certainly too full of mud to be of any use, but finding it somehow gave him the courage to ease himself carefully on to all fours.

"I'm coming, Percy."

Slowly he inched his way through the mud until he could hear the wounded man's moaning all too clearly. He edged himself towards the sound.

"Where are you hit, Percy?"

"Legs!"

"I can't see anything. Is it bad?"

Only laboured breathing told him that Percy Hood was still alive. Gingerly he stretched out and touched the other man. Still there was no response. Apprehensively, he moved closer and ran his hands down to where he expected the legs to be . . . and to his relief found that both were intact. In the darkness it was impossible to tell whether either leg was badly damaged. The sticky wetness could have been blood or just the slimy mud of Flanders.

"Hang on, Percy. It'll be light soon and we'll get the stretcher-bearers out for you. They'll patch you up and have you back at the field hospital in no time at all."

"Don't leave me, will you?"

"Of course not. Where the hell do you think I could go?"

"I'm scared, Ben."

"You're not the only one, Percy."

"Are you really frightened?

"Frightened? I'm bloody terrified."

"I want to go home."

"You will, lad. I think you've got yourself a one-way trip back to Blighty."

"Is it long until morning, Ben?"

"No . . . not long."

For the rest of the night the two farmers' boys from Ambridge – both of them still well short of their twenty-first birthday – lay huddled together in the Flanders field, saying nothing . . . but holding each other's hand.

Phoebe Archer had been staring out of the window towards the village and thinking about her boys. She could feel the tears prickle in her eyes when she heard heavy steps in the yard. She quickly pulled herself together and went to the kitchen door to greet Frank, her third and youngest son, who had been out in the fields since dawn.

"Do you want something more to eat, Frank?"

"No, thanks. I'm not that hungry."

"But you didn't eat very much breakfast."

"No . . . but I'm not hungry."

"Well, what have you come in for? You haven't finished out there yet, have you?"

"No . . . I wanted to have a chat."

Phoebe went cold. Frank was fast approaching his nineteenth birthday and she dreaded what was coming next. He was going to join up, too.

"What about?"

She desperately tried to keep all the emotion out of her voice.

"You know . . . the war, and joining up. The army, all that."

"Yes."

"Well, I'm sorry . . . but I don't want to go to France. I don't want to be a soldier like Ben and Dan."

Relief swept over Phoebe Archer. She wanted to hug her son, but she knew that would have flustered him. She looked at him in silence.

"That's all right then, Frank."

She smiled gently.

"No, it's not."

He shuffled uncomfortably.

"You don't understand. Everyone will think I'm a coward, especially Dad."

"Don't be daft . . ."

She started to argue, but she suddenly realised that young Frank was almost certainly right. People would think he was too scared to join up. But surely not his father? Not John?

"Have you talked to your dad about it?"

"Not yet . . . but I know what he's going to say. He's so proud of Dan and Ben that he's bound to tell me I'm a coward. But I'm not, Mum. Honestly, I'm not frightened to go off to the war. It's just that I don't want to fight anyone. It all seems such a waste."

Before his mother could answer, the door opened and John Archer came noisily into the kitchen.

"What's up here, then? Nobody got any work to do?"

Phoebe looked at him reprovingly.

"Frank and I were just having a chat."

"Oh, aye. What about?"

"The army . . ."

"I see. It's your turn to become a hero, is it, lad?"

Frank flinched.

"No, Dad. I don't want to be a hero. I don't want to go to France. I don't want to be a soldier."

A look of fear mingled with bewilderment came over John Archer's face. He was a man of few words at the best of times; now he was all but speechless.

11

"I don't understand."

"He's not a coward, John."

"Didn't say he was. What is it, lad?"

"I can't explain, Dad. I've just made up my mind that I'm not going to fight and that's that. I don't care what you think. I'm not going into the army."

"Hang on a bit, lad. Nobody's saying you have to do anything."

"I'm going to emigrate instead."

"Emigrate?"

"To New Zealand. I know I can get a job there on a sheep-farm. Bert Lily knows a bloke from Penny Hassett who's got relatives out there and he says they're always looking for workers."

John looked long and deep into his youngest son's blue eyes. He was satisfied with what he saw. There was a deep sadness but no trace of fear. This son was no more a coward than his other two lads were. They had shown their courage by joining up. Young Frank had a different kind of courage.

"Right, lad. If that's your decision, it's all right by me. It's your life. Your mother and I can't lead it for you. When will you be leaving?"

"I don't know."

"Soon?"

"Probably."

"Right, then. Let us know when you've got it all fixed up. Say if you need any money or anything else."

"Thanks, Dad."

Relieved, Frank turned away from his parents and went off back to the fields. He knew neither of them would ever understand his feelings, but he was glad they could accept them.

John turned to his wife. He could see that the tears weren't far away from her eyes.

"Don't worry, lass. We've still got each other."

He put his strong arms around her and they stood there in the middle of the big farmhouse kitchen saying nothing, thinking of faraway places . . . France,

Flanders, New Zealand . . . and they held each other very tightly.

CHAPTER TWO

The mail orderly was always the most popular man in the camp . . . with those for whom he brought letters from home. At the headquarters of the Sixteenth Battalion of the Borsetshire Regiment "somewhere in France" everyone else tried to ignore his existence. No one wanted to be reminded that yet another day had come and there was no letter from sweetheart, wife, mother or even sister.

For weeks, Daniel Archer had deliberately busied himself around noon when the mail was due. He hated the agony of waiting and the fear of disappointment. Letters were always handed out in alphabetical order, and he was therefore among the first to know that there wasn't one for him. That meant he had to slink off to his billet when the As were finished, half hoping that the orderly might have got it wrong and that his letter would turn up under some other initial . . . but too embarrassed to stay and betray his distress if it didn't.

He had been in the army for two years now, and knew only too well that the postal services were at best sporadic. He knew that the absence of letters in the camp didn't mean that no one had written to him. He kept telling himself that . . . but he didn't seem to hear, and spent hours of misery wondering why no one seemed to care about him.

The day's delivery had just been made. As usual there was no letter for him. As usual, he was lying disconsolately on the thin palliasse that served as his bed. Coming from a close-knit family and a small village where everybody knew everything about everybody else, he couldn't easily come to terms with this complete lack of information.

What was happening back on the farm? Were his parents coping without him and Ben? What about young Frank? Had he, too, joined up? What about Ben? The last he'd heard he was supposed to be somewhere in Flanders, and that was where some of the heaviest fighting was said to be taking place. Was he all right? Was he even still alive?

More agonisingly, what about Doris Forrest?

Before he had joined up and left Ambridge, he had set his cap at young Doris, daughter of the local gamekeeper. He wasn't exactly sure how she had responded because they had both been very shy and inexperienced . . . and she was barely past her sixteenth birthday at the time. He thought she liked him as much as he liked her, but she had never actually used any terms of endearment. Mind you, neither had he.

When the time had come for him to leave Ambridge she had not been to see him off at the station at Hollerton Junction. She had said that it was an occasion for families only, but he had thought that was just an excuse. In the end he had been glad she wasn't there because he felt sure he would have burst into tears. During their own private goodbyes she had been quite restrained, and again he had been glad because it allowed him to maintain his outward courage and coolness. She had said she'd write, though, and that had to be a good sign.

In two years he'd received only three letters from her, and none of them had given anything away about any feelings she might have for him beyond simple friendship. On his part, he had started to write to her on countless occasions, but he couldn't remember how many letters he had finished and posted; nor could he remember what those he had sent had actually said. He wasn't very good at writing. He had left school at thirteen and what education he'd had up until then certainly hadn't included learning to write love letters.

After two years of separation, he couldn't honestly say how he felt about Doris. He thought about her a lot . . . but that may have had more to do with the awful circumstances under which he and his mates were contriving to survive. Did thinking about her simply help him to keep his mind off what was happening all around? Was she really so pretty as he recalled, or was his memory supplying the picture he wanted?

He might have come up with some of the answers if his reverie hadn't been shattered by the appearance of the corporal.

"Get yourself upright!"

"Sorry, Corporal."

"You will be if you don't get down to the stables at the double. The CSM is after your blood. There's another shortage of hay for the horses and he reckons as how it's all your fault."

This was nothing new. Daniel felt relieved that he wasn't in more serious trouble. He was responsible for hay procurement for the whole regiment, and that meant trying to persuade local farmers to part with some of their precious supplies. As he didn't speak a word of French and none of them had more than a few scraps of English, there were often communication problems, and that sometimes meant that the odd load of hay didn't materialise as he had thought promised.

The company sergeant major always took such hiccups badly. "It was for the sake of a bleeding horse that a whole bleeding empire was lost," was one of his favourite sayings. He always bellowed it at the top of his voice, presumably for the whole bleeding empire to hear.

With his farming background – and a lot of patient sign-language – Daniel was usually able to sort out the problem and persuade the French farmers to respond with some urgency.

When he got to the main stable block, CSM Grundy was almost purple with rage.

"These bloody Froggie friends of yours have done it again! You know that it was for the want of a bleeding horse that a bleeding empire was lost! Well, if you don't get something to feed our horses – and damn quick, too – we'll have lost this bloody war!"

"Sorry, Sergeant Major."

16

"I don't want your bloody apologies, lad. I want my bloody hay. Get it. Now!"

"Do you know what loads haven't turned up, Sergeant Major?"

"What? Are you asking me? What do you think I am? I am the company sergeant major, not a bloody clerk! It's your job to know these things. Now . . . get knowing . . . otherwise I'll feed you to the bloody horses. Understand?"

"Yes, Sergeant Major."

Daniel couldn't help grinning as the sergeant major strutted away. He had known him as plain George Grundy when they had played cricket together for the Ambridge village team, and he remembered him leaving the field in exactly the same outraged way whenever he had been bowled out.

"What are you smiling about?"

It was the mail orderly.

"Nothing, really."

"Well, I've got an item that will make you smile for something."

"A letter?"

"Aye . . . a letter. From a woman . . . and she isn't your mother!"

Doris Forrest sang happily to herself as she made some last-minute adjustments to the little white lace cap that she had pinned to the top of her dark curls. It wasn't quite six o'clock, but already the summer sun was pouring through the tiny window of her bedroom and the dawn chorus had become a clamour of birdsong.

Very shortly she would have to go downstairs to be at the beck and call of the mistress, but these few minutes first thing in the morning were her very own and she cherished them. Because she always slept like a top she had no difficulty in getting up. That had not exactly endeared her to the other kitchen maids when she'd had to share a room with them, and she had taken to feigning tiredness so as not to upset them. Now, as lady's maid to Mrs Lawson-Hope, she had her own little bedroom and she didn't have to worry about that any more.

Looking out over the beautiful gardens of the Manor House she could see the little clump of cottages that clustered around the green at Ambridge and, a little way beyond that, she caught the glint of the sun reflected on the gently flowing waters of the River Am, which had given the village its name. From her high vantage point she had a view right across to where Farmer Archer's sheep were grazing on Lakey Hill. That was one of her favourite walks . . . up the hill, across Three Barrows field and on to the path of the old Roman road that went straight through Leaders Wood.

Doris hadn't been on that or any other walk for ages because she had been so busy learning all about her new job which required her to look after the every need of the squire's wife. She'd worked at the big house for more than four years, but it was only a month or so earlier – on her seventeenth birthday – that Mrs Cooper, the housekeeper, had told her she was being promoted from the kitchen to become lady's maid.

She'd been frightened to death at the thought of being in Mrs Lawson-Hope's company all the time and having to do everything absolutely correctly. But from the very start Mrs Lawson-Hope had been nice to her and had quietly explained how she liked things done.

Somewhere downstairs Doris heard a door bang and that startled her out of her reverie. Smoothing down her apron and checking her black dress for bits of fluff, she picked up the piece of paper that listed her duties for the day. She didn't really need to, but she glanced quickly at the note: 6 a.m. – Light fire in dining-room and then take hot water to mistress's bedroom.

The big clock in the hall was striking six as she opened the great door into the elegant dining-room.

Mrs Cooper was already in there, checking the plates and dishes on the long Tudor sideboard.

"Good morning, Mrs Cooper."

"Nearly didn't make it on time, Forrest. Couldn't you get yourself out of bed?"

"Oh no, Mrs Cooper. I was up in plenty of time."

"Just get on with it, then."

Mrs Cooper hadn't wanted to promote her when Sally Blower had left to go to another job. Her favourite had been Lisa Scroby, and she had been barely civil to Doris since Mrs Lawson-Hope had overruled her. Lady's maids were not supposed to do menial tasks, but insisting that young Forrest looked after the dining-room fire was Mrs Cooper's way of reasserting her authority.

Once she'd got the fire going, Doris went to the kitchen to fetch the huge jug of hot water that her mistress expected to be in her bedroom by half-past six every morning, summer and winter. It was one of her least favourite jobs. If the water was too hot it was very difficult to carry it up the three flights of stairs. If it wasn't hot enough Mrs Lawson-Hope would be displeased. She never actually complained, but she became slightly less charming for the rest of the morning and that was admonishment enough.

This morning, Doris Forrest reckoned she had got it just right and she knocked on the bedroom door and called out a cheerful "Good morning." To her surprise, Mrs Lawson-Hope was already up and about.

"Good morning, Doris. Did you sleep well?"

"Yes, thank you, Mrs Lawson-Hope."

"I'm afraid I didn't. I've been tossing and turning all night."

"I am sorry, ma'am."

"You know my husband is due home today?"

"Yes, Mrs Lawson-Hope."

Mrs Lawson-Hope didn't like being called ma'am and she'd asked that the servants use her name at least on every other occasion they had to address her.

"I do so hope he makes it. I miss him so much. Are any of your family in the war, Doris?"

"No, ma'am."

William Forrest, her father, was the gamekeeper on a neighbouring estate, and for some reason unexplained to her hadn't joined up when most of the other men in the village had enlisted. Her little brothers, Teddy and Tommy, were too young.

"You're very lucky, my dear."

When war had been declared, Squire Lawson-Hope had been the first man in the whole of Borsetshire to volunteer. He had to set a good example, he said. A few months after he'd gone, his two elder sons, Cedric and Hugh, had followed that example. All were now serving somewhere in France. There were several other boys from Ambridge out there, too . . . Percy Hood, George Grundy, Bill Sawyer, John Plant and, of course, the two Archer brothers, Daniel and Ben.

Young Doris blushed guiltily when she thought about the Archers. She had stepped out with both of them at different times and couldn't make up her mind which of them she preferred. Daniel, she thought, was very nice . . . a bit shy and quiet, but always very interesting when he talked about the countryside and how he was going to make such a good farmer when he was older. Ben, on the other hand, was much more devil-may-care and had always made her laugh and giggle when they had walked out together. He never talked about farming.

She felt bad when they had gone off to the war. Her father had refused to let her go to Hollerton Junction to wave farewell to Daniel because, he said, she was much too young. A year later, however, he hadn't minded when she went to the station with Mr and Mrs Archer to see Ben off, but then she had let everyone down by blubbering like a baby just before the train steamed out.

Both of the boys had written to her and it was clear even from their short letters that neither knew about the other's interest in her. She knew that was wrong, but she didn't know how to put things right. Sometimes she thought she owed more loyalty to Ben. He was nearer her age and with all those tears at the station, he was entitled to think she liked him a lot. But she didn't have the heart to tell nice, gentle Daniel that she liked his younger brother so much. She knew that would hurt him and she didn't want to do that. She didn't want to hurt either of them.

She had replied to one of Daniel's letters because somehow she found it easier to write to him. She knew he wouldn't laugh at her childish scrawl or worry about whether or not she put the punctuation marks in the right places. She could imagine Ben showing her letter to all his pals and she would have hated that. At the same time, she knew she ought to write to him. It was the least she could do for someone who was showing his bravery by fighting for his country.

She wished she could talk to Mrs Lawson-Hope about her worries. She was bound to know what was the best thing to do. Right now, however, it was clear that she had too many other things on her mind.

"I get very frightened every time someone comes to the door. I always imagine they're going to bring me bad news about the squire or Cedric or Hugh. Do you mind me talking to you like this, Doris?"

"No, Mrs Lawson-Hope, of course I don't."

"I feel so ashamed, you see. I sit around feeling sorry for myself and thinking how much I have to suffer the loneliness and the anxiety of not knowing what's happening to them. It's so selfish when they are out there facing death at every turn."

"Are they really facing death?"

Doris was constantly overhearing scraps of conversation about the war and the bravery of the lads at the Front – whatever that was – but very little of it really registered with her. She had never thought about anyone she knew ever being killed.

"Oh it's not just the fact that they could be killed that frightens me, my dear. They could be horribly mutilated from bullet wounds or shrapnel and their lungs could be badly affected by this awful new gas the Germans are said to be using. What if any of them were to come home without a leg or an arm or even an eye? Or what if their lungs were so badly damaged that they could hardly breathe without terrible pain? What if all the carnage they've witnessed affects their minds?"

Mrs Lawson-Hope was very close to tears and Doris felt very embarrassed. She had never seen an adult crying before and didn't know what to do. Her natural instinct was to put her arms around the older woman and try to comfort her, but she couldn't possibly do that with her employer. Instead she became practical and matter-of-fact.

"Would you like me to bring your breakfast upstairs this morning?"

Mrs Lawson-Hope recognised the problem she had created for her young maid and quickly pulled herself together.

"No, thank you, Doris. It's very kind of you, but please tell Mrs Cooper that I shall be downstairs at seven-thirty as usual."

The stiff upper lip of the landed gentry was back in place, and Doris Forrest, so close to being a confidante and friend of the squire's sad wife, was once more the lady's maid . . . a servant, albeit a trusted one.

CHAPTER THREE

Colonel George Lawson-Hope looked wearily at the piece of paper on his desk. More bad news. Nothing shocked him any more, none of the grim information that constantly crossed his desk. Three months ago, Cedric, his elder son, had been killed by enemy gun fire in Flanders. Then he had learned, only a few days ago, that young Hugh had been seriously wounded and was in a field hospital somewhere up near the Front. No, the war had produced too much pain, too much savagery, for anything new to affect him.

He knew, however, that young Daniel Archer would be shattered by the news that he was going to have to break to him.

"Get me Lance-Corporal Archer," he called to his orderly.

"Sir!"

Private William Evans hurried off to the stable block where he knew he would find young Archer helping with the battalion's horses.

The colonel sat in his makeshift office and remembered how his poor wife had responded when he had told her about Cedric's death. The War Office had been very decent about it and had given him leave to go home to tell her himself. She had just sat there, very pale, and seeming to take it quite well. Only he knew how much she was hurting underneath. Now she was a broken woman who, he knew, spent almost every day expecting to hear that either Hugh or he himself had been killed.

He had asked Hugh's commanding officer not to notify his wife of their second son's wounding in the hope that he would be able to get back again to tell her himself. He prayed that the news wouldn't reach her in any roundabout way. There were so many Ambridge lads involved in the war that it could get back via one of them.

Bringing himself quickly back to the unpleasant business in hand, the colonel reflected on the sad irony of farmer John Archer's death. While his two sons had so far managed to survive the worst ravages of the war, he had fallen and died in the lush, green fields of Borsetshire.

There was a tap on the door and Lance-Corporal Archer came in and saluted smartly.

"You wanted to see me, sir?"

"Yes, Daniel. Sit down."

This was only the second time the young man had been in the colonel's office and he was disconcerted by the use of his Christian name and the invitation to sit down. He knew he was about to hear bad news. The troops had been told they would be posted to Flanders any day; this, assumed Daniel, was the moment of truth. His brother had been in Flanders all summer, and from the reports he'd heard it was a hell-hole.

Colonel Lawson-Hope cleared his throat and looked down at the piece of paper on his desk.

"It's bad news . . . about your father, I'm afraid."

"My father?"

Daniel couldn't understand. Had his father, too, joined the army? He'd heard nothing from home for months so anything could have happened. Had his father been sent to the Front and been wounded already?

"Yes, Daniel, your father. He's dead."

"Dead? But I didn't know he was even in the army. How did it happen?"

"No, no, Daniel. Your father wasn't in the army. He died at home in Ambridge."

Daniel's shoulders sagged and his face went white.

"I don't understand, sir. Was there an accident?"

"No. He had a heart attack while he was out in the fields. He died before they could get him to the hospital, I understand."

"When did it happen?"

"Last week . . . the seventh of October."

24

"The seventh? What's the date today, sir?"

The colonel knew that people often tried to stave off the shock of bad news by concentrating on irrelevant details.

"It's the fourteenth."

Daniel sagged even further in the wooden chair and he let his head drop as he covered his face with his hands. Tomorrow was his birthday. He would be twenty-one . . . and entitled to call himself a man for the first time. Today? Well, today he felt more like a frightened rabbit.

"Will I be able to go home for the funeral, sir?"

"It's too late for that, unfortunately. Your father was buried yesterday. I'm afraid the message took rather a long time to reach us. I'm sorry. But you're to go home. There'll be no more war for you. You'll need to look after your mother and, of course, the farm is your responsibility now."

"The farm?"

"Yes . . . and I hope you don't mind, but I've taken the liberty of asking one of my men from the Manor House to keep an eye on things until you can get back there."

This was no longer a conversation between colonel and soldier. The squire was fulfilling his responsibility to one of his tenant farmers.

"Thank you, Squire. That's very good of you."

Farmer Daniel Archer pulled himself together. This was no time to feel sorry for himself. If he were going to have to shoulder new responsibilities then the sooner he knuckled down to them the better.

"When will I be able to leave, sir?"

"Just as soon as we can get the paperwork sorted out. If you see Evans on the way out, he'll explain all the necessary arrangements."

"Thank you, sir."

"This time next week, Daniel, you'll be back home in Borsetshire."

The Second Battalion of the Borsetshire Regiment was moving up the line behind a Canadian Pioneer company from Ypres towards the Passchendaele Ridge – another target that somebody in the War Office had decreed must be taken at all costs. It was only a five-mile march, the officers had said.

It may have been an honest five miles as the crow flies, but then crows don't fly along a narrow pathway that zigzags and corkscrews through fields of mud. The Borsetshires had been on the move for more than four hours, picking their way across a long snake of duckboards and desperately avoiding the great craters that pocked the landscape. They were still nowhere in sight of their objective. Not that anyone had been deceived by the officers' information. It was a long, long time since any soldiers had believed anything they heard about this bloody war. Once, in their innocence, they may have been cheered by suggestions that it would soon be over. Now, anyone daft enough to even hint at an end would be in serious danger of losing his front teeth.

Ben Archer had drawn the short straw for this half-crazed stumble through the desolate fields. Everyone was expected to carry extra equipment during an advance, but it had fallen to his lot to shoulder a heavy machine-gun. It was bitterly cold, and at times the wind threatened to sweep him off the narrow path, but he could still feel the sweat rolling down his back.

Even when they stopped for rest he couldn't take the gun off his shoulders. There was nowhere to put it. The duckboards were too narrow, and if he had put it down anywhere else it would have disappeared into the thick, black mud.

Somewhere behind him a New Zealand howitzer crew suddenly started firing over the British and Canadian troops in the general direction of the German lines. The shells whined overhead more or less at random. It was obvious that the Enzees were trying to relieve their boredom again.

"Hell," thought Private Archer, "that will only make Fritz bloody angry."

26

He was right. Within minutes the Germans were sending down a barrage of heavy shells that crashed and exploded all around the Borsetshire position.

A few yards away, one of the battalion commanders, Captain Winstanley, bawled out an order.

"Everyone down!"

But self-preservation already had every man flat on his belly within a fraction of a second of the first shellburst.

In his prostrate position, Ben was pinned under the weight of the heavy machine-gun and couldn't move.

"Give us a hand, somebody. This bloody gun's going to cut me in half!"

"Shut up and stop moaning, Archer!"

Captain Winstanley had no sympathy for any of his men who seemed to have no stomach for the fight. By this stage of the war there were plenty of soldiers who bitterly regretted ever having volunteered. Private Ben Archer wasn't one of them, and the officer's snarled comment hurt him only because of its unfairness.

He felt a hand slip between his aching shoulders and the barrel of the gun, easing the weight for a few seconds.

"Don't say anything, matey, or we'll have that bastard acting like he's on Fritz's side."

Despite the agony of his position, and the erupting shells all around, Ben grinned. His old pal Percy Hood showed as little concern for jumped-up officers as he did. Although they both came from Ambridge and had joined up together, they hadn't really known each other very well until a couple of months back when Percy had been wounded in the leg. After tending to him, Ben had carried him all the way back to a field hospital for treatment and the chance of a well-earned ticket back to Blighty. However, Percy had turned up again only a couple of weeks later, sporting a slight limp, having refused to take the option to go home. Since then, the two men were almost inseparable.

"I reckon our Mr Winstanley thinks he's still back on his country estate pushing the Borsetshire peasants around! Hang on a jiffy and I'll have that load off your back."

"Percy, be careful, for God's sake. We don't want to lose the gun. I think we're going to need it where we're going. Don't you?"

"Aye. But we've got to get there first. Loosen the webbing . . . now wriggle backwards while I take the weight."

"What do you two men think you're up to?"

Captain Winstanley had crawled towards them and was peering at them through the swirling smoke.

"Just gathering ourselves for the final onslaught of the enemy positions, sir."

It was a model answer from the Old Soldier's handbook. The young officer acknowledged defeat by crawling away without another word.

Relieved of the terrible weight, Ben lay back for a few minutes and eased the pain across his shoulders and back. He almost blessed the German gunners for bringing him this relief.

A few minutes later he knew that Captain Winstanley was back in command of the situation.

"Right, let's move. We've got to keep up with the Canadians and we won't do that with our faces in the dirt. Move!"

"I'll take that gun for a spell, Ben boy. You take the ammunition bags."

Percy Hood gingerly slung the heavy weight across his narrow shoulders as he sat in a crouching position . . . and then found that he couldn't straighten up.

"Hell's bells. I reckon you must have got half the ruddy battlefield stuck up the barrel of this thing. It weighs a ton. Give us a hand!"

Just as the two friends managed to struggle to their feet, another shell exploded close by and a great shower of mud blasted across them, throwing Percy off-balance. The heavy machine-gun slid off his shoulder, thumped on the wooden duckboard, toppled over the side into a shell-hole and disappeared from sight beneath the black, muddy water.

Whatever he might think about officers and gentlemen, Percy was still a very good soldier and he would have plunged into the freezing, stinking water after the gun if Ben hadn't grabbed hold of him.

"Don't be daft, Percy. It's gone. There's no way of getting it out of there."

Further argument was avoided by yet another explosion, closer than ever. The shell had scored a direct hit on the duckboards behind them, opening up a great crater. It would take the Pioneers hours to create a new way around it for the rest of the battalion to follow.

"That's done it, Percy. Our last line of retreat's gone. There's nothing else for it. We'll have to press on and be bloody heroes!"

"Do you think Winstanley will give us the chance? I reckon he'll court martial us and order us to be bloody well shot in the field for losing that machine-gun!"

Was that another one of Percy's jokes or was he being serious?

"You're probably right but I don't think we need worry . . . until we get to Passchendaele or whatever hell we're supposed to be going to!"

CHAPTER FOUR

Peace on earth, good will towards all men . . . the single bell of St Stephen's church rang out across the mist-shrouded fields, calling the villagers of Ambridge to a special Christmas morning service.

For four long, weary years the bell had been muffled and all celebrations subdued by the war. Now it was over. Six weeks before the Armistice had been signed. Already all the local boys who had been in the army were back home . . . all those that would come home.

For Squire Lawson-Hope and his wife, the service would be one of remembrance. They had lost both their sons in the war, and the squire's service in France had ruined his health. Still proud in the uniform of a colonel in the Borsetshire Regiment, he presented a brave figure to the world as he leaned heavily on his walking-stick and acknowledged the greetings of his tenants and neighbours.

At his side, his wife managed to smile warmly at everyone. Few would have imagined her recovery possible from the double tragedy of her sons' deaths. After the news about young Cedric had been broken she had taken to her bed for weeks, and everyone had been so worried about her reaction to a second blow that they kept Hugh's death from her for as long as they could. But it had been the uncertainty of not knowing their fate that had caused her most anguish. Once she had learned the worst, she was able to show tremendous fortitude, and it was her support and strength that had helped her husband regain his own will to live after his breakdown in health.

George, their youngest son, had been too young to join up, but he had basked in the glory of his brothers' part in the war, and had even been able to see their deaths as something heroic. Since the Armistice he'd had to develop his own particular courage in coming to accept that he must live in their shadow and always be measured against what they might have been.

The three of them were followed into the family pew by Mrs Lawson-Hope's personal maid, Doris Forrest. She would have much rather been with her own family on this special day, but when the men of the family were away in the war she had sat with her mistress in church and she hadn't liked suggesting anything different just yet.

As usual, she had been up since before six o'clock, and had been very disappointed when she'd looked out of her window and seen that it wasn't snowing. She had been longing for a white Christmas and the chance to build snowmen and have a snowfight with her father and her little brother, Tommy. She would finish work at the Manor House immediately after the traditional Christmas dinner there and then would join her own family's celebrations. Robbed of the chance to go tobogganing on Lakey Hill, she would try and persuade everyone to go for a long walk later on.

Sitting in the squire's pew at the front of the church was additionally frustrating for Doris as she couldn't see what was going on behind her, and she daren't turn around to have a look to see who was there. As the squire moved forwards to read the first lesson she desperately wanted to turn and have a quick peep. But she suffered in silence and sat there as demurely as was expected of her.

She knew the Archer family would be in the church somewhere – her mother had told her that Mrs Archer had never missed a service since her husband had died. Doris blushed, as she always did when she thought of the two Archer sons.

Daniel had been home for more than a year, but because he was now running Brookfield Farm and she didn't get very much time off from the Manor House, she had seen him only six or seven times. She didn't think she could say they were sweethearts, but she had thought things were going quite nicely in the right direction . . . until Ben had come home only a few weeks earlier.

She remembered his homecoming very well. Mrs Lawson-Hope had given her the afternoon off to go down to the village green to join the crowd that had gathered to give him a hero's welcome. Still in his uniform, Ben had jumped off the cart before it came into sight of the village and, accompanied by the band and half the village children, he had marched the last half-mile with tremendous swagger.

Everyone had said how handsome he looked . . . and Doris agreed. They all said how fit he looked, but she thought his face was a bit gaunt and he was awfully pale, especially against the ruddy outdoor faces of the other menfolk. She'd been very surprised – and flattered – when he noticed her among the crowd and had immediately thrown his arms around her and given her an enormous hug. She was also surprised at how much she had enjoyed feeling his arms hold her so tight. It had left her very confused . . . Ben or Daniel?

Perhaps she'd be able to make up her mind this evening when, her father had told her, both boys and their mother would be joining in the Forrests' traditional Christmas Night party at the lodge. She blushed again, this time in anticipation.

From several pews back, Daniel Archer had an excellent view of Doris Forrest's dark curls swirling out from underneath her tiny hat. She looked very pretty, even from behind. He had tried to hurry his mother when they'd been getting ready for church, in the hope that he could have a quick chat with Doris before the service started, but they'd arrived at the church door just in time to see the squire's party file into their pew. He'd have to wait until this evening and hope that he could have a few minutes with her alone during the party.

There was a lot Daniel wanted to say to her. He wanted to ask her to marry him – not that he would do that tonight, of course – but he wanted to arrange to talk to her father, and he felt he ought not to do that until Doris had agreed that he could. He didn't quite know how he was going to approach the subject, but Christmas was as good a time as any.

Daniel knew about her mixed-up feelings for him and his brother. Doris had told him about Ben when he himself had got back from the war, and he had been on the green with the crowd to welcome Ben home, and had seen them together. He had understood how easily she must have been carried away by the emotional return of the conquering hero. He didn't think those feelings would last. In fact, they had probably worn off already.

Certainly, he didn't think his younger brother was in love with Doris. They hadn't actually spoken about it, but since he'd been home young Ben had stepped out with several of the local girls. He was much too restless to want to settle down with a wife yet.

Daniel, however, needed a wife. His mother was a great help in running the farm, just as she had supported his father, but she must be nearly forty-five and, in any case, it wasn't right for a man to have to rely on his mother. He was twenty-two now and really ought to start thinking about raising a family of his own.

He had mentioned that to Ben, but Ben had just laughed and made a sarcastic comment about Dan needing someone to pass the farm on to. Ben had actually been quite a problem for his brother since he'd come back from the war. He didn't want to help around the farm, but he didn't show any signs of finding another job either. Knowing what he had been through in Flanders, Daniel did not want to press him too much for the time being, however. Despite the way Ben seemed to have changed since they'd gone away, Daniel was still very fond of his younger brother.

Sandwiched in the pew between her two elder sons, Phoebe didn't join in with the hymn-singing. She was thinking of her third boy, Frank. He had gone off to

New Zealand only a few days before John had died, and at first she'd been very angry with him as if, somehow, her husband's death had been Frank's fault for not staying on to do his share of the work. All that had passed now, and she kept wondering how he was faring so far away from home.

She had no idea where New Zealand was. Somewhere on the other side of the world, even further away than France. The two letters that were all she'd received from him so far had taken months to reach Ambridge, and they weren't exactly brimful of information. All she really knew was that he'd found himself a job and had got over his homesickness.

Hopeless as it was, Phoebe's Christmas wish was for the family to be reunited. She wondered if there would ever be a time again when they would all sit around the same fireplace at this special time of the year. Shocked at the sadness of her thoughts, she decided to count her blessings. Looking at the two sons sitting with her, she suddenly felt very grateful. She smiled.

Sitting alongside his mother, who kept embarrassing him by holding his hand, Ben was feeling edgy, not the least in the mood for Christmas. While he was there, he'd thought he'd hated every minute of army life, but now he wasn't so sure. Certainly, he would never willingly go back into action, but he missed the camaraderie he'd found in the battalion.

Since Percy Hood had gone off to work at the bakery in Borchester there was nobody left in Ambridge he could have a proper conversation with. Everyone else in the village seemed happy to tug their forelocks to the gentry, and they were all blinded to the fact that the horrors of the war had been the fault of the politicians. That kind of blind servility made him angrier than ever.

Why couldn't they see? The thousands of soldiers who had died unnecessarily weren't just anonymous figures – they were their brothers and sons. And what of those who'd survived? Were they just to be heroes for one day and then forgotten the next? Maybe young

Frank was right. Maybe he'd be better off trying to make a new life for himself in the colonies. There they didn't have peasants and masters.

In his sermon the vicar talked about the great sacrifice of those who had fallen. He praised the magnificent courage of those who had sustained terrible wounds in action against the enemy. He gloried in the splendid fortitude of those who could only stay at home and wait for their loved ones to return.

Across the aisle, Ben could see Major Godfrey Winstanley sitting proudly at the end of his family pew. He was wearing the dress uniform of the Borsetshires, with the fine ribbon of the Military Cross and all his other campaign ribbons above the breast pocket. He could afford to look pleased. His decorations were the spoils of war for the gentleman soldier.

Ben had nothing to show for all his long and arduous service. He had never been subservient enough to the officers to get promotion. Three times he'd had to take command of his troop when all the officers and NCOs had been killed, but he didn't get even a single lance-corporal's stripe out of it. In action, he had been as brave as the next man . . . braver than many, he would say. There had never been any mention in despatches for him.

He had actually saved Winstanley's life when they had stormed the Passchendaele Ridge. The young officer, still a captain then, had almost walked on to a German bayonet. He had been grateful enough to Ben then, but since they had returned to Ambridge he hadn't bothered to say a single word to him. Maybe if Ben had taken over Brookfield Farm instead of his brother, it might have been different?

Would it make any difference to Doris Forrest, now sitting there looking pleased with herself among the landed gentry, if he were a farmer instead of just his brother's labourer? She seemed quite interested in him, but she seemed a lot more interested in his big brother and, no doubt, in his big brother's very comfortable farmhouse. Still, it was worth a try. She could only say no.

After the service there was the usual disorder outside the church as everyone tried to wish everyone else the compliments of the season. The squire congratulated the vicar on his sermon. The vicar said how glad he was to see the squire back in the village. Mrs Lawson-Hope thanked the vicar's wife for making the church look so pretty. The vicar's wife told Mrs Lawson-Hope how pleased she was to see the squire back in the village.

Ben watched in amusement as his brother finally gave up hope of catching Doris Forrest's eye. She was too busy gossiping with several other girls to notice him.

"Ben . . . do you have a moment?"

It was Godfrey Winstanley.

"Pardon?"

"Do you have a moment? I'd like you to meet my wife."

Ben was taken aback. He didn't know how to react, so he fell back on military discipline.

"Good morning, Major."

His arm almost whipped up into the old soldier's salute.

"No, no. No rank, please."

Now it was Godfrey Winstanley who was embarrassed.

"I told my wife about what happened at Passchendaele. You know – the business with that bayonet I didn't see. She said she'd like to thank you."

Mrs Winstanley stood quietly at her husband's elbow, blushing slightly.

"I'm terribly grateful to you for saving my husband's life. It was very brave of you."

Ben was lost for words. The landed gentry were not often publicly beholden to ordinary folks.

"Well . . . merry Christmas to you both!"

CHAPTER FIVE

Like the three wise men following the star, Phoebe Archer and her two sons wound their way across the fields towards the happy sounds of Christmas celebrations coming from the gamekeeper's lodge on the Winstanley estate. It was a lovely, starlit night and, with a sharp frost making the ground underfoot rock hard, they'd decided to take the short cut rather than walk around by the road.

Everything looked sharp and clear in the eerie light of the moon, and their feet crunched on the frozen grass. The leafless trees were outlined in silver hoar. In the distance the gentle slope of Lakey Hill could be clearly seen as they paused to watch a small animal streak across the silver ground.

There were lamps at every window of the house, and even at two hundred yards they could hear the deep bass voice of William Forrest leading his family and friends in a lusty rendering of "Oh Come, All Ye Faithful". Another group was approaching by the pathway from the road, but the Archers couldn't make out who they were.

"He's got the timing right."

"What do you mean, Ben?"

"Oh come, all ye faithful . . . we're coming!"

Phoebe smiled at her son. It was so good to have him home. He was always making her laugh with his little comments.

"It's a pity we're farmers and not shepherds. Then we could have brought the Forrests some gold and frankincense and myrrh."

Even Daniel laughed.

"Silly beggar! It was the three wise men who brought gifts, not the shepherds."

"Yes, of course . . . the shepherds were probably typically tight-fisted. Still, I expect the Forrests will be satisfied with our little Christmas gifts."

All three of them laughed. When they knocked on the door they were welcomed by William Forrest himself, looking slightly uncomfortable in his Sunday suit.

"You're just in time to join in the carol-singing, and then Lisa will get us all a bite to eat."

In the parlour the Forrests had already been joined by several other families, and the big, comfortable room was crowded and noisy. Ben was still in jocular mood.

"Looks like half the village are here, Mr Forrest. I hope it's the right half!"

"Aye, young Ben. We always have the right folk in our house at Christmastime. See you behave yourself!"

William Forrest was very proud of what had become one of the traditions of the Ambridge Christmas. As a gamekeeper he needed to carry some authority, and one of the ways he had tried to do that was to make himself and Lisa prominent in the life of the village. It had been hard going at first because there was a natural suspicion of gamekeepers, and Lisa, who had been in service as a scullery maid, was very shy. However, they had both persevered and had succeeded. This was their sixteenth Christmas party, and over the last ten years, at least, no one had been known to refuse an invitation. Everyone who regarded themselves as anyone was there this evening. No wonder William bade Ben Archer to behave himself.

Ben had been trying to spot Doris, but she wasn't in the room. He did, however, see Sally Blower and she was a very good substitute . . . nearly as pretty, a bit older and a bit more experienced. With a wink at his elder brother, he eased his way through the noisy crowd towards her.

"Hello, Sally. I haven't seen you in years. Are you still working in Borchester?"

Before she could reply, Mr Forrest announced that the next carol would be "While Shepherds Watched Their Flocks By Night". Further conversation was impossible so Ben slipped his arm round Sally's shoulders and they both joined happily in the singing.

More persevering than his young brother, Daniel Archer found Doris in the kitchen, where she was helping her mother cut a great pile of sandwiches and cold meats.

"Evening, Mrs Forrest . . . Doris. Happy Christmas to you both."

"Daniel Archer . . . it's lovely to see you. I'm glad you were able to tear yourself away from Brookfield for five minutes. Here, would you mind giving our Doris a hand while I go and check that there's plenty of mulled ale left?"

"Oh, aye. I suppose so."

Daniel was surprised to have such an early opportunity to talk to Doris, and now that it had come he wasn't so sure it was a good idea. He felt a bit flustered.

"What do you want me to do, Doris? I'm not very good at cutting bread."

"Well, you can't stand there looking like a great awkward lump. Try putting the sandwiches on to plates."

Awkward was precisely how he felt . . . but not about the bread. He was too worried about the exact words he should use without making a fool of himself. It should have been so easy. He'd practised it often enough in his mind.

"Doris . . ."

"Yes, Daniel?"

All the carefully considered preamble disappeared from his head.

"Doris, do you see us as sweethearts?"

There was a great thump and the kitchen door flew open. Mrs Forrest came back carrying two empty jugs.

"The ale's fine, so off you go, Daniel. The kitchen's no place for a man. You can go too, Doris. I'll finish these things off myself. Thank you for your help, Daniel."

The opportunity gone, his question unanswered except by a shy, non-committal smile, Daniel Archer

39

reluctantly pushed his way back into the crowded parlour. Doris followed him. They were just in time to hear Mr Forrest declare that it was time for "party pieces". Everyone groaned in mock despair. Some of the solo performances were already well known around the district and their highly variable standards only added to the amusement.

Usually, it was Mr Forrest who began this part of the evening with a quite tuneful rendition of an old local folk song called "The Village Pump". But instead of standing up to sing, he announced that he had a special surprise up his sleeve.

"Young Tom has been practising his performance for some weeks now and I reckon that such dedication deserves special attention. If none of you minds, I'll ask him to get things going for us tonight."

Little Tom Forrest shuffled forward, looking very nervous. His elder brother Teddy covered his face with his hands and groaned loudly, but everyone else tried to encourage him.

"What are you going to do, Tommy? Recite?"

"No. I'm going to sing."

"Sing? What are you going to sing?"

"I'm going to sing 'The Village Pump'."

There was a great roar of laughter, which the poor lad didn't understand. He didn't know his father had been singing the same song for as long as anyone in the village could remember, nor that it was now always met with friendly derision. Undaunted, he ploughed on and sang every single verse and was rewarded by great cheers when he had finished.

As the evening's entertainment unfolded, Doris found herself being pursued by both the Archer brothers. It was all very flattering, but she was beginning to get a bit worried. She had known that Daniel had been about to get quite serious in the kitchen, and she had been relieved when her mother had interrupted them. At eighteen she felt she was still too young to get serious about anyone . . . although at

40

the same time she didn't want to say anything that might make Daniel go away.

Nothing, though, would make Ben go away, it seemed. He had appeared very interested in Sally Blower when Doris had first spotted him – at least, they were involved in a long conversation, and she'd felt she was interrupting something when she'd gone to have a word with Sally. Since then, however, Ben had tried to persuade Doris to stand under the large bunch of mistletoe hanging from the centre of the ceiling about half a dozen times, and she wasn't sure how many more times she'd be able to fend him off. It was thinking about how to keep him at bay that finally made up her mind for her. She realised that she preferred Daniel Archer!

Unaware of this development, Daniel was becoming increasingly uncomfortable. He was quite shy and didn't mix very well, and it was hard work trying to keep up a conversation without going on and on about the problems of running Brookfield Farm. He reckoned people must be bored with all his worries. Since Lisa Forrest had thrown him out of the kitchen, his attempts to have another word with Doris had all been thwarted. Several times it was his own brother who interrupted them. Was he being mischievous or was he, too, serious about Doris? He'd have to tackle him about it at some point.

At eleven o'clock the party began to break up. Most of the menfolk present had to be up at the crack of dawn, and after the plentiful supplies of mulled ale they'd supped, they would need a good few hours of sleep.

Daniel was helping his mother to find her shawl when he saw Ben trap Doris under the bunch of mistletoe. He had his arms wrapped tightly around her and was kissing her full on the lips.

Sensing the anger mounting in her eldest son, Phoebe decided to intervene.

"Come on, Ben. We have to be going home now. We must let Mr Forrest get to his bed."

It had little effect. Ben continued to kiss Doris as the others in the room laughed nervously. Daniel didn't laugh at all. He watched grim-faced until he could bear it no longer.

"Right, Ben. That's more than enough. Leave the lass alone. Let her breathe for heaven's sake."

He grabbed his brother by the shoulder and pulled him away from the breathless girl, who stood blushing and looking very confused. For a few seconds the brothers glared at each other. Ben was the first to turn away.

"Sorry, Doris. No harm meant. I thought you and I had a bit of an understanding. If I was wrong, I apologise."

Doris smiled in relief. Her father, only half aware of what had happened, put his arm around her shoulders protectively.

With only the barest of polite farewells to Mr and Mrs Forrest, Daniel strode out into the night, leaving his mother to do a proper job of thanking them for their hospitality. Halfway across the frost-covered fields, he realised his brother was still back at the lodge. He wanted to go back to make sure he wasn't still pestering Doris, but he knew he couldn't do that without making everyone even more embarrassed.

When he got home to Brookfield, Daniel was still angry. Uncharacteristically, he banged about the farmhouse, nearly knocking over one of the lamps. He went to his room and lay down on the bed fully clothed. Somehow he reckoned that he wasn't going to sleep very well.

Lying there with his stomach churning, he heard the others come back. After a few minutes he listened as his mother came quietly up the stairs and went to bed. Downstairs, his brother moved noisily about the kitchen. Glancing at the clock in the corner of the room as he leaned across to put out the lamp, Daniel saw that there was still a quarter of an hour left of Christmas Day.

A few minutes later there was a tap on the bedroom door.

"Dan? Are you still awake?"

"Aye."

"You and I need to talk."

"Come in, then."

"No, not up here. We'll keep Mum awake."

Daniel got up and followed his brother downstairs to the kitchen. The coals gleamed dully in the huge range and Daniel automatically went across to rake them over. Ben watched him in amusement.

"You really are domesticated. You don't really need a wife if you can look after yourself so well."

Daniel spun around, all the anger in him boiling up again. He had assumed that his younger brother wanted to apologise for what had happened, but it was clear that Ben wasn't in any mood for saying sorry.

"I'm not sorry about kissing Doris Forrest, you know."

"Well, you damned well ought to be!"

"Why? Are you and she sweethearts? She never told me she was your girl all the other times I kissed her."

Daniel had no idea whether or not his brother had really kissed Doris as often as he claimed, but the very thought of it made him feel jealous.

"Stop it now, Ben. I've had enough."

"You've had enough? What do you mean, you've had enough?"

Ben stood in the middle of the kitchen, swaying slightly. His face was flushed with too much ale, but his eyes were still bright with anger. Daniel decided to try to reason with him.

"You know you don't care about Doris. She's just another girl you want to add to your list of conquests. Why can't you leave her alone? She's too nice a lass to mess around."

"Conquests? There aren't any conquests in this life for ordinary folk like us. Didn't you learn anything from the bloody war? Don't you know that there aren't any winners? You and I didn't win any war. We were just lucky enough not to be among the losers who died."

"Let's just talk about Doris."

"What's the matter? Are you afraid to talk about the war? Are you ashamed to talk about how cushy it was for you in France . . . a million bloody miles from danger?"

Daniel had often felt guilty about not seeing action in France, but it really wasn't his fault. He'd never gone out of his way to avoid it.

"I went where I was sent. I was ready to go to the Front with you. I didn't ask to be posted to the regimental headquarters."

"No, but I bet you were happy there . . . hiding behind your bloody haystacks!"

From the rising pitch of his voice, Daniel knew there was never going to be anything like a reasoned discussion, but he felt he ought to go on trying.

"I thought we were going to talk about Doris Forrest?"

"All right, let's talk about her. You say I don't care about her. How do you know what I care about? You've never bothered to ask me. Do you really know what Doris wants? Have you ever asked her? Do you think I couldn't make her happy? Do you think she wants to be a boring farmer's wife?"

"Stop it now, Ben. For God's sake, please stop it!"

"Sure . . . stop because you want to stop. Just like I'm not supposed to kiss Doris because you don't want me to kiss her. Just like I'm not allowed to be a farmer because you don't want me to be a farmer."

"What are you talking about, lad? I don't want to stop you being a farmer."

"Lad? Lad? Damn you, Dan Archer, I'm not a lad any more. I'm a man. Can't you see that? Haven't I proved that? They called me a man soon enough when they were looking for men to join up. I was a man all right when they sent me in to fight the Germans. Why's it so different now? Why can't you see me as a man? Well, I am a man! I want to lead my own life. If I want to go out and enjoy myself every now and then, why

44

shouldn't I? If I want to kiss Doris Forrest, why shouldn't I? If I want to be a farmer, why shouldn't I? Haven't I earned that right just as much as you have? What was the lousy war about if it wasn't to ensure a better future for people like me? That's what they told us but, of course, it wasn't true. It was all a bloody great con trick by the politicians. That's what it was!"

The torrent of bitterness shocked Daniel, and he was equally shocked by the realisation that his brother was right. He didn't really know what Ben thought about anything. They'd hardly spoken since he'd come back from Flanders. Daniel had been too concerned with his own problems.

"Look, lad . . . sorry . . . Ben. I am sorry. I've been very busy with the farm since Dad died."

"Yes . . . busy feathering your own nest. Busy digging yourself into Brookfield while I was digging trenches in Flanders . . . busy laying cosy plans for you and Doris Forrest to set up together as man and wife. I bet you were hoping that I'd be one of the thousands who didn't come back."

"That's not fair. I never thought any such thing!"

"It would have been a lot easier for you if I'd got killed with all the other lads."

The younger brother swayed again and looked as if he might lose his balance. Daniel moved forwards and put his hand out to steady him.

"Take it easy, Ben. Let's both calm down."

What happened next would remain with Daniel Archer for many years. As he stepped forwards, Ben swung a tremendous punch that caught him full in the mouth. The force of it knocked him against the kitchen table, which slid noisily across the tiled floor. He clutched at it for support and stood there feeling dazed. Looking in bewilderment at the anger in the other man's eyes, he was surprised by the taste of his own blood. The last time he had been in a fight was in the school playground when he was about twelve, and no one had drawn blood on that occasion.

If Daniel thought that was an end to the nightmare, he was wrong. His brother moved towards him menacingly.

"That's it, Danny boy! There's no way back for you and me. This is the parting of the ways. There's no room for both of us at Brookfield. We've got to see this thing out."

In disbelief, Daniel backed away.

"Don't be stupid, lad."

He dodged as another blow was aimed at his head and he half stumbled against a chair.

"What's the matter, Danny? Haven't you got the stomach for a fight? Still frightened of a bit of action, are you?"

"That's got nothing to do with it. I don't want to fight you."

"No, of course you don't. You don't want to get hurt. You're just another coward like young Frank."

"Only an idiot would want to get hurt, and you know Frank isn't a coward. You found out about the stupidity of the war the hard way. Young Frank didn't need to join up to learn that. You know how much courage it must have taken for him to say he wouldn't go. You know he's not a coward so stop talking nonsense!"

"Yes, Danny boy, let's both stop talking. Put up your fists and fight like a man."

Angered by the remarks about Frank and with his split lip now uncomfortably swollen, Daniel decided that there was no other way out of the situation.

"Right. If it's a fight you want, it's a fight you can have . . . but not in here."

He pushed past his brother, out through the kitchen door and across the yard to the big barn. Now he was very angry, not only with Ben but also with himself for having allowed things to get so out of hand.

The blackness of the barn was relieved only slightly by the moonlight shining through the doorway. Back in the house, the grandfather clock struck midnight. Christmas Day was over. No more good will towards all men . . . no more good will between brothers.

In the murky gloom the two men faced up to each other. Daniel Archer – short, thick-set and clearly unsure of himself – stood with his two fists under his chin in the way he vaguely remembered from watching the bare-fisted boxers in the travelling fairground. Ben Archer – slightly taller, lean and very confident from a dozen fights during his army service – kept his arms by his sides.

"What do you want, Dan? Is it to be Marquis of Queensberry rules, then?"

He grinned wickedly and suddenly lunged forwards, hitting Daniel full in the face with his right fist. As his brother staggered back he followed up with a crunching body blow that sent Daniel tumbling to the ground.

Feeling as if he had been kicked by a horse, Daniel lay on the straw-covered floor, looking up at the younger man with a mixture of hurt and anger. He started to get up, but was sent crashing down again when his brother's heavy boot thumped into his ribs. He could feel blood coming from his damaged nose, and the cut on his lip had opened up wider.

This time he rolled well clear of his brother before getting unsteadily to his feet. Now he knew that Ben was right. Their different war experiences had driven them apart. They couldn't live together at Brookfield.

"Okay, Ben. You win. You've proved your point. If being a grand fighter makes you a man, you're a man . . . but now what? You can't stay here any more. What will you do?"

"What will I do? Don't you mean, what will you do? Don't you know that the winner takes all in prize fights? What do they say? To the victor, the spoils? My spoils will be Brookfield . . . and Doris Forrest!"

"Don't be so daft. You can't just do that. Besides, you yourself said there were never any winners in a conflict."

"I've just changed the rules. That's what the politicians do. I'm the winner. I take everything."

Daniel wasn't sure if his brother were still drunk or if he meant what he said. He couldn't understand what was going on. He hurt all over and now he was also very frightened. If Ben were serious, Daniel couldn't simply accept that his whole future had been wrecked by a couple of unfair blows.

"If that's the way you want it, Ben, you'd better put up your fists again."

This time it was Daniel who struck the first blow. He punched Ben in the ribs and then in the midriff. The reply was yet another blow to his battered lip, but now he hardly noticed the pain. Any inhibitions he might have had about fighting his brother disappeared. All he felt was anger. He remembered the hours he had spent working on the farm while Ben had gone off to enjoy himself.

It had been like that when they were boys and were supposed to be helping their father, but it had got worse when Ben had got back from the war. There was no doubt about it – he was a lazy beggar, and now here he was demanding that he should take over Brookfield.

A staggering blow to the side of the head sent Daniel on to his knees but he grabbed his brother around the waist to make sure that he didn't get another kick in the ribs. His weight knocked him off balance and they both rolled on the floor, grappling with each other and trying to get their blows in. Daniel broke clear and scrambled to his feet.

Ben's face was now as badly marked as his brother's. The effect of the ale had worn off and he was stone-cold sober. He could only barely remember how the fight had started, but he knew that it had been his fault. Ben also knew that it was he who had set the stakes. He felt very guilty. He had always liked and respected his elder brother. His disgruntlement wasn't a family affair at all.

He was angry and bitter with a society that had allowed the politicians to send hundreds and thousands of men to their deaths in some unnecessary war. Why had he taken it out on his brother? Why had he said that about Frank being a coward? Of course it wasn't true. Frank wasn't scared about fighting. He just had more sense than most other people.

What about Doris? Well, he did like her a lot . . . but then he liked two or three other girls a lot, too. He knew in his heart that Doris saw herself as Daniel's girl. He had been a bit jealous, that was all.

What about Brookfield? He didn't really resent Daniel's being given the tenancy. That was the tradition in the countryside, and he didn't really see himself as a farmer anyway. He had hated having to spend hours in the fields leading the horse while his father was behind the plough. And after the excitement of army life, he couldn't see himself settling down to life on the farm.

He felt Daniel drag him to his feet and then he staggered as another series of punches hit him in the face and body. He was learning a few new things about his big brother. He certainly packed a powerful punch. A right hook caught him on the side of the head, and he crashed back to the floor with a great ringing in his ear. For a second or two Ben wanted to leap up and retaliate, but enough was enough. Whatever had been the reason for the fight was now gone. He lay still and kept his eyes shut, pretending to be out cold.

He felt his brother bend down and get hold of him, but this time he wasn't dragged upright. Instead, he was lifted up quite gently and carried back to the farmhouse, then eased down into the big armchair by the range.

Daniel looked at his brother's battered face with concern. What sort of madness had caused all this? He hadn't wanted to fight and now he couldn't believe that he had caused so much damage. The blood around his own cuts had congealed as he went to the pump and soaked a towel in cold water. Gingerly, he began wiping his brother's face. He flinched as he saw a deep cut over the left eye. Ben stirred and looked up at him.

"Take it easy, Ben. It's all over. There's no more fighting for either of us."

"Aye, you're right, as always, Dan. It *is* finished. You've won fair and square. Everything is yours now . . . to the victor, the spoils . . . remember?"

"Don't say that. Nobody's won anything."

For a few moments the brothers looked at each other. There was nothing either could say.

"Let's go to bed now. We can talk in the morning."

From upstairs they heard their mother call to them.

"Are you lads all right?"

The brothers looked at each other again. Ben grinned.

"Yes . . . we're both fine!"

Daniel wasn't so sure, but he managed to smile through his bruised lips as he followed Ben up the stairs. They both went to sleep almost immediately.

In the morning Daniel eased himself out of bed as the damage of the night before engulfed him in pain. His ribs were badly bruised and his left knee was swollen. As he stepped off the rug on to the cold floor and did his usual little jig from foot to foot, his left leg gave way under him. He sat on the floor trying to work out what hurt most. His lip felt the size of a turnip, and he could hardly see out of his right eye. Putting on his shirt and trousers was causing agony, and he had to sit on the edge of the bed to get his breath back. The clock told him he should be out and about but his body screamed to go back to bed. Marshalling all his willpower, he limped downstairs to the kitchen. Even lighting the lamp was a struggle, but at least it was much warmer in the kitchen where the range had stayed lit all night. He went across and opened the iron door and let the heat wash over him as he raked the ashes. It felt good. Looking at the clock, he was horrified to see the time but, late as it was, he put the kettle on the hob. He badly needed a cup of tea.

The hot, sweet liquid made him jump as he sipped it through cracked lips. He had to force himself to drink it, but by the time he had finished it he was beginning to feel a little more human. Looking out of the window he could see that the frost had been sharp overnight, and he shivered at the prospect of going out into the cold. He'd need an extra pair of socks under his boots. Across the yard he could see that the barn door was open. The thought of last night's nightmare made him groan. He would never understand how it had happened.

He heard footsteps on the stairs, and his mother came into the kitchen. She looked at his bruised face. She didn't say anything, but turned to stare out of the window. He realised she was close to tears.

"It's Ben, now. He's gone, too. Just like Frank."

"Gone?"

"In the middle of the night. He woke me up to say he had to leave. He asked me to say goodbye to you and to say he was sorry . . . for everything."

CHAPTER SIX

Doris Forrest watched as a butterfly flew haphazardly across the garden of the Manor House. With nothing better to do than enjoy the warmth of the summer sunshine, she lay back on the grass and propped up her head on her hands. She followed the butterfly's zigzag flight and tried to guess which flower it would alight on next. She giggled quietly to herself as she got it wrong each time.

She loved these kind of afternoons. Mrs Lawson-Hope enjoyed pottering around in the garden, and whenever she got out the flower basket and the cutters she encouraged Doris to change into a summer frock and sit outside for the odd hour or so to get some fresh air.

She could see her mistress now, bent over a rose bush at the far end of the garden, and she could hear the occasional sharp snipping sound as Mrs Lawson-Hope gathered flowers for the house. Later she would show Doris how to arrange them. So far, Doris had been given dozens of lessons, but she had never actually been allowed to do any arrangements because Mrs Lawson-Hope enjoyed it too much herself. Doris lay back again to soak up the sun.

A shadow fell across her and she looked up. The tall, handsome figure of George Lawson-Hope towered over her. In a baggy white jacket and a broad-brimmed straw hat, he looked very much like his late father.

"Hello, Doris. Enjoying the sunshine?"

"Yes, Master."

"Please, Doris, don't call me that. You know I've asked you to call me George."

Doris smiled at him shyly.

"Yes, I know that, but it's very difficult, sir."

She laughed nervously at her further formality.

"It's no good, Doris. You know, the Labour Party will never get elected if people like you don't learn that people like me are just human beings. The chains will never shake loose by themselves. It's you who's got to throw them off."

Doris had no idea what he was talking about. She had no knowledge of politics and even less interest.

"It just seems polite and proper to call you 'master' or 'sir' when I talk to you. I try to do as you say, but I always feel as if I haven't finished my sentence or something, and my dad is always telling off our Tommy for not finishing his sentences."

"Never mind, Doris. It doesn't matter very much. It's just that you make me feel positively ancient. We're more or less the same age, and you treat me with the kind of respect you usually reserve for older people."

George always felt slightly hurt when the village girls failed to respond to his attempts at friendliness. They seemed so suspicious all the time; he could never understand why. The days of the Sir Jasper-type landlord had long since gone . . . even before his father had become squire. Surely everyone knew that? Whatever the reason, the result was that he was restricted to a very small circle of associates. He found it all very frustrating. He didn't much care for some of the daughters of the landed gentry who were constantly being paraded before him . . . no doubt as possible brides. They were all pretty brainless and terribly vain.

Now, someone like Doris Forrest was much more appealing. He didn't get many chances to talk to her, though. She always seemed to be so busy, chirruping around the house; he knew she was quite bright, too. He really would like to get to know her.

"I don't suppose you'd care to come for a walk with me? It's such a lovely day that I thought I'd go up over Lakey Hill and out on the Penny Hassett road. It'd only be for an hour or two, and we'd be back in plenty of time for tea."

Doris glanced towards the rose garden, where her mistress was still busily snipping flowers. She was longing to go for a walk and would have accepted without hesitation – but Mrs Lawson-Hope liked to change into a clean dress when she'd finished gardening.

"I'm sorry, sir, but I have to attend to the mistress very shortly."

Even as it came out, she wanted to bite her tongue. She knew she was sounding very stiff and formal, and she knew that would probably hurt him. That's the last thing she wanted to do. She liked the young man very much, and would willingly have stepped out with him under normal circumstances. She wondered if she ever really would be able to drop the "sirs" and "masters" and the "madams" and "mistresses". She would have dearly liked to suggest another time for the walk, but she thought that would appear much too forward.

The young man blushed and smiled gently.

"Don't worry, Doris. I understand perfectly. Forgive me for making the suggestion."

As he walked away across the garden towards the house, she wanted to call him back. She wanted to say that he didn't understand, and she wanted to explain to him that she really did have to go back to work in a very short time. Sadly, she decided it was pointless. She was, after all, only his mother's lady's maid.

"Doris, I'm going inside now. Will you come to help me change?"

If she hadn't known better, the girl might have thought that Mrs Lawson-Hope had perfectly timed her reminder of Doris's position.

"Was that George going off for his afternoon walk?"

"Yes, Mrs Lawson-Hope."

"How did he seem? Was he cheerful?"

"Yes, I think so."

Doris wondered what her mistress was getting at. She wasn't sure if Mrs Lawson-Hope minded George being friendly with the servants.

"He didn't say very much, ma'am. He just mentioned that he was going for a walk over Lakey Hill."

They walked together across the lawn in silence, and it wasn't until they'd climbed the stairs and were in Mrs

Lawson-Hope's beautiful dressing-room that the conversation re-started. Mrs Lawson-Hope seldom said very much to Doris in front of the other servants. She preferred to chat in the privacy of her room.

"Lakey Hill, did you say? Isn't that one of your favourite walks?"

Doris blushed.

"Yes, it is, but I haven't been there for some time."

"Why's that? I haven't been keeping you too busy, I hope?"

"Oh no, ma'am, it's not that. I just haven't felt like going."

The truth was that no one had asked her to go and at the age of twenty she would have been too embarrassed to go by herself. All her girlfriends were already going steady, and she was beginning to feel that she might have been left on the shelf. She couldn't bear to be teased about it, so she'd often used the excuse of being busy.

"Do you ever hear from young Ben Archer?"

Doris was startled by the unexpectedness of the question.

"No . . . I haven't heard of him since he left the village eighteen months ago."

"Isn't he in Canada?"

"I believe so, ma'am."

"And his younger brother is in New Zealand?"

"That's right, ma'am. My dad says they both have the wanderlust. Neither of them would ever have been happy in a small place like Ambridge."

Doris felt slightly angry whenever she thought about Ben Archer. At that Christmas party he'd been very friendly, much too forward if anything, and yet the very next morning he'd gone without saying a word of farewell to her or anyone else in the village. At first everyone said it was because she'd spurned him, but she'd denied it so often that people now seemed to believe her.

"I sometimes think a spell abroad might be the best thing for George."

Mrs Lawson-Hope was clearly in a talkative mood. Doris paused as she laid out the fresh dress for her. She sometimes felt sad that her mistress obviously had very few people to chat to and needed to confide in her maid.

"Why do you think he should go abroad? Don't you need him here?"

"Oh yes, I need him very much. I dread to think how we could manage the estate without him."

"What is it, then?"

"Well . . . he just seems so restless since his father died, and I do think he's much too young to have all this responsibility. I also think he's too hard on himself, trying to make up for the two brothers he lost in the war. Do you understand, Doris?"

Doris understood much better than Mrs Lawson-Hope could ever imagine. She hadn't seen Daniel Archer in over a year because of the war and what it did to people! She didn't, however, feel very much like talking about it.

"No, Mrs Lawson-Hope, not really."

"He's such a sensitive young man, you know. He feels guilty that he inherited the estate instead of Cedric, who would have done so as the eldest son if he'd come back from Flanders. He also feels very guilty that he doesn't want to do things the way his father did them, and yet that's only natural for someone with an independent mind."

Doris wondered if that had anything to do with the young master's recent comments about chains and politics and a new social order or something. It was all too confusing for her, and she knew she couldn't help any more. She had also finished laying out Mrs Lawson-Hope's clothes for the rest of the afternoon and for the evening.

"If that's all, Mrs Lawson-Hope, I ought to go downstairs and check that Mrs Cooper doesn't need any help. She mentioned earlier that she might, because Lisa Scroby was feeling very poorly and would probably have to go to bed."

"Of course, Doris, you carry on. Thank you very much."

There was nothing for Doris to do in the kitchen. When she got back to her own room she felt guilty for not having stayed to talk to Mrs Lawson-Hope.

Her guilt was increased when she reflected on how much the Lawson-Hopes had done for her and how ungrateful she must sometimes appear. She wasn't very good at expressing her feelings, but she really was filled with gratitude towards them.

When Doris had left the village school at the age of thirteen there had been nothing else for her to do but go into service. Her father had only just got a position as an assistant gamekeeper and there was very little money for a growing family – he'd have had to struggle to feed them all properly if it hadn't been for the rabbits and birds that came from the estate. When Doris had first gone to the Manor House as a scullery maid, she had not been able to believe the huge amount of food that was prepared in the kitchens every day.

Doris was aware that a number of her friends often went hungry, and she remembered little Ned Larkin at school saying he didn't know why he bothered going home for his dinner because he hardly ever got any. He said he could tell as soon as he went in the house whether or not there would be anything to eat. If there were, the tablecloth would be folded away and there would be some bowls on the table; otherwise the tablecloth would still be on and he'd be lucky to get a piece of bread and dripping.

Ned was a great one for exaggerating, and you could never be sure when he was telling the truth. But Doris could see for herself that his clothes were always heavily patched, and the cottage the family lived in was in a pretty bad state of repair. The windows were always broken, and once when she'd been in the kitchen she'd noticed a hole in the ceiling that you could see through into the room above.

Although the cottage her family had lived in then was smaller than the gamekeeper's lodge they now lived in, it was always clean and comfortable, and her mother kept the fires going all year round. That meant endless trips to the woods for kindling and logs, but at least the house was usually warm. When Doris had started work at the Manor House, she wasn't at all sure at first that she was any better off than she'd been at home. She'd been used to helping her mother with odd bits and pieces of housework and cooking, but now she suddenly found herself with an exhausting routine of chores to get through every day that kept her going from six in the morning until nine at night.

She had to start the day by sweeping out the main entrance hall. Then came the task of lighting the fire in the big dining-room, ready for the squire and his family to come down to breakfast. She had ten minutes for her own breakfast in the kitchen before rushing upstairs to help serve breakfast and then clear away all the dishes.

After that, it was a long round of getting rid of the morning slops and cleaning out the wash-stands, making beds, lighting more fires, getting in coal and wood, helping with lunch, washing dishes, cleaning the silver and mopping the red tiles in the kitchen about a dozen times every day. Mrs Cooper was a great stickler for keeping the place clean, and would call for the floor to be mopped almost every time anyone walked across it. In the evenings Doris had to turn down all the beds, light the lamps, draw the blinds and eventually take hot water around all the bedrooms.

She used to be happy at the end of her long day to tumble into her own bed exhausted, but she'd never minded the hard work. There had always been plenty of time in the day to gossip with the other girls in the kitchen, and that was one of the things she did miss now as the lady's maid. The younger girls regarded her with a certain amount of awe and suspicion, and they would seldom chatter when she was around. Doris hoped she wasn't coming to be regarded in the same way as Mrs Cooper was, with everyone terrified of her presence.

Maybe it was time she thought about leaving service and trying to find another job. No, she couldn't do that. Mrs Lawson-Hope needed her. She was only just out of widow's mourning. Having to train a new personal maid would only add to all her burdens. That wouldn't be fair, on top of everything else.

A month earlier Doris had accompanied Mrs Lawson-Hope to the unveiling of the war memorial in the village square by Mr Winstanley. She'd never seen such sadness. The memorial bore all the names of the local men who had died in action. At the top of the list was Mrs Lawson-Hope's eldest son, Cedric, killed in action at the Battle of Messines. Next came her other son, Hugh, who had been wounded at Passchendaele and died a month later in a field hospital.

The late squire's name wasn't on the memorial, so history would not record him as a war hero, and other people would forget him in time. But Mrs Lawson-Hope could never forget. Her husband had gone to the war and survived his two sons, but he'd paid a heavy price. He had been caught in a gas attack that had left his lungs badly damaged and his health seriously impaired – the very fate that Mrs Lawson-Hope had feared most for him. He had come home a sad, broken figure who suffered terrible physical and psychological pain. At first he had tried desperately to return to something like a normal life, but when he saw that was never going to be possible he had started handing the reins over to young George. Barely more than a year after helping to win the peace, he had died – unheroically – in bed.

Having seen all that Mrs Lawson-Hope had gone through in those months, Doris knew she would remain with her for a while yet. She'd probably stay on until she got married . . . that's if she ever did! Doris was beginning to have serious doubts about that as well.

Her mind drifted back to Daniel Archer. She was sure he'd been going to ask her about getting married at that

Christmas party where Ben had given her that little spot of embarrassment. Daniel had got as far as asking if she considered them to be sweethearts, but then they'd been interrupted and he'd never raised the subject again. After his brother went off so unexpectedly, Daniel had called to see her and had apologised for taking her for granted. She didn't know what he meant by that and she'd not got the chance to find out because he had become even more shy and awkward than usual and had left hurriedly without saying another word.

She had seen him around the village on several occasions since then, but he had not been anything more than civil to her. When she'd noticed that he even avoided coming to the Forrest Christmas party this year she'd assumed that he had found another girl, and had been expecting to hear that he was getting married. But the village gossips hadn't so far linked his name with anyone else's. That in itself was odd because with his hundred-acre farm Daniel Archer was regarded as one of the most eligible men in the village – and, as a result, a target for wagging tongues.

Just then came a tap on her bedroom door. One of the young kitchen maids had been despatched to tell her that Mrs Cooper would be obliged if she could come downstairs to lend a hand with the preparations for tea.

Further thoughts about Daniel would have to wait.

CHAPTER SEVEN

At last Brookfield Farm was beginning to look the way Daniel Archer wanted it, and he allowed himself the rare luxury of feeling proud. It wasn't quite three years since he'd been brought back from France to take over the farm on the death of his father, but already he'd got all hundred acres in hand. Now he felt he had earned the title of Farmer Archer.

It had been an uphill struggle, though. His father had been ill for longer than anyone realised and the farm was in a very poor state when Daniel took it over. Several fields of grass had gone to seed, and all the equipment was in need of repair or replacement. Furthermore, the cows had been poorly fed, and the milk yield had been very low. There had been times when Daniel had despaired. If it hadn't been for his mother and some of his neighbours, he might have given up.

The squire's agent had been very helpful, and Daniel had been able to call on any of the surrounding farmers for the loan of tools when needed. Even George Grundy had been willing to lend a hand. As his sergeant major in the army George had given Daniel a very rough ride while they were serving together in France. At the end of the war he had gone on to serve in Palestine, but then, to everyone's surprise, he'd left the army and come back to Ambridge to take up the tenancy of Grange Farm. He'd turned out to be a very good neighbour as far as Daniel was concerned.

Daniel hadn't really known what he was doing in those early days. He'd simply blundered on as best he could – sometimes with disastrous consequences. On one occasion a wheel had come off the corn-drilling machine, and when he'd put it back on he'd somehow managed to damage the spike barrel. Halfway through the drilling, one of the spikes flew off and slashed the hind leg of the horse. The poor animal had been so badly hurt that Daniel had had to have it put down, and he'd been unable to borrow another one to finish the drilling because every farmer in the district was using their own for the same purpose.

In the end Walter Gabriel had come to his rescue. Walter, who'd been in the same class as Daniel at school, owned a bit of a smallholding down nearer the village where he kept a few animals and some chickens and had half an acre of potatoes; he must have been one of the few men in the village not involved with planting crops at the time. Daniel had bumped into him in The Bull, where he'd gone looking for help. Walter had responded by volunteering not only his own services but those of Annie, his wife, as well . . . although she, poor girl, didn't know it at the time.

Walter was a dab hand at cobbling things together, and he managed to convert the horse-harness so that all three of them – Walter, Daniel and Annie – were able to pull the drilling machine across the field with Daniel's mother guiding it. For three long days they had dragged it backwards and forwards, ignoring the pain from their blisters and bruises. It had been back-breaking work, but they had completed the planting only a day and a half later than it would have been done with the horse-drawn drill.

That year's harvest had been saved. As it turned out, it was an especially good one and Daniel had been full of gratitude to Walter and Annie. They had remained the best of pals ever since.

Now, looking over his twenty acres of corn turning gold in the late summer sunshine, Daniel had cause to feel pleased with his efforts. The old corn-driller had been replaced by a machine so big that it had to be pulled by two horses, and that had nearly halved the time needed for planting, so that he'd been able to plant a few acres of new grass for grazing and hay-making. He'd also been able to mark out a couple of fields for winter wheat and barley, and soon he'd be getting ready to sow them.

His mother, who worked almost as many hours as Daniel did himself, had created a very big kitchen garden where she grew potatoes, sprouts and cabbage in large enough quantities to supply half the village. The noisy hens that strutted around the farmyard were also her responsibility, and egg sales were now beginning to show a healthy profit.

Next year, Daniel was planning to expand his small dairy herd. He already had sixty head of Friesians and, all being well, he intended buying about twenty followers that would join the herd when they were ready. Soon he might be able to think about taking on a man to help out; that, he hoped, would take some of the weight off his mother's shoulders.

He worried about his mother. She worked around the farm as hard as any man could, and she looked after all the domestic chores as well. He suspected that she enjoyed it all only because it stopped her having too much time to think. Once or twice he'd seen the brave face she showed to the world slip, and he knew she'd been thinking about Ben and Frank.

Phoebe hardly ever spoke about Ben, but she talked quite a bit about young Frank who seemed to have settled down well in New Zealand where he'd got himself a decent job on some huge sheep-farm – more than two thousand acres, he'd said. In his last letter he'd written about a new girlfriend, Maria Gibson. Daniel and his mother suspected it was quite serious because she'd been mentioned by name four times!

Daniel smiled to himself. He couldn't picture his little brother thousands of miles away, working on the farm and going out with girls. The last time he had seen him had been in 1916, when Frank had been a skinny, fresh-faced teenager not long out of short trousers. Like Daniel and Ben at the same age, he had worked around Brookfield but had not had the strength to be of much help even though he had always shown willing. Now he was almost twenty-one and, by all accounts, was as much a man as any of them.

Daniel always felt ashamed when he thought about his other brother. He would never forget that awful night in the barn when he and Ben had laid into each other with such venom. It wasn't so much the physical damage he'd inflicted on Ben that bothered Daniel; that was only part of the story. He could still remember the Boxing Day morning that followed as clearly as if it were yesterday. When his mother had told him that Ben had gone away from the farm forever, he had felt enormous guilt and remorse.

Daniel had gone over it all a thousand times in his head since. He knew that he had treated Ben badly when he came back from Flanders. He had never bothered to ask Ben if he wanted to talk about his war experience. He had never stopped to think how Ben might have been affected by all the horrors he had seen. Obsessed by his own problems, it never occurred to him to ask his brother for help – that could probably have solved everything. If he'd only invited Ben properly to come to work on the farm with him, they could have made a great partnership.

The business over Doris Forrest need never have happened either. Daniel had always taken it for granted that he would eventually marry her, but he'd failed to mention the fact to Doris, let alone to his brother. If he had done so, he was certain that Ben would never have pestered Doris and she would never have encouraged him. As it was, Daniel had managed to lose both of them because of his thoughtlessness.

Ben was somewhere in Canada now, but that was about all they knew. He had sent only a couple of postcards since he'd left Ambridge. The first was from Southampton, saying he was taking a boat to America and that he intended going on to somewhere near Vancouver to look for a job. Although the second postcard had Canadian stamps on it, the postmark wasn't very clear and Ben hadn't given any address, so they had no idea where he was. Nor did they know yet if he ever got a job. They'd heard nothing further in over a year.

Daniel knew well enough where Doris Forrest was. She was still at the Manor House and doing very well there, by all accounts. She seemed quite a favourite of Mrs Lawson-Hope's, and on the odd occasions he'd caught sight of her in the village she'd looked fine . . . as pretty as a picture, in fact. Although he had never heard any stories linking her with another man, Daniel couldn't believe she wasn't stepping out with one of the lads at the big house. He was really quite surprised that she wasn't married by now.

Daniel had gone to see her just once after Ben left. He had tried to apologise for causing her any embarrassment and for taking her for granted, but she hadn't seemed very bothered so he had kept out of her way ever since. Several times he had thought about going to see her again to try to patch things up, but each time he had run out of courage and had done nothing.

"A penny for them, Daniel."

"Pardon?"

He hadn't heard his mother come out of the farmhouse and cross the yard to join him as he leaned against the fence that kept the cattle out of the stream running alongside the field.

"I'm sorry. I was miles away."

"I know you were, lad. That's why I was offering such a vast reward for your thoughts. I thought I might get a very cheap trip out of it."

"Well, just at that moment I wasn't all that far away."

Phoebe Archer knew instantly what was on her son's mind. He'd been thinking about a wife once again.

"Still got young Doris Forrest in your sights, have you?"

"No, of course not. That was all over a long, long time ago, I'm afraid. But I was just wondering to myself if she'll be getting herself married soon."

"Married? Who to? I didn't know she was stepping out with anyone, and I'm pretty sure Lisa Forrest doesn't know either . . . at least she didn't when I spoke to her only last week."

"Hang on, Mother. Don't go starting any rumours. I didn't say the girl was getting married. I said I was wondering."

"Why were you wondering that, Daniel? Why don't you know? I thought you and Doris were going to be sweethearts at one stage. Whatever went wrong between you?"

"It's a long story, Mother."

Except for the brief exchanges with Ben during the fight, Daniel had never talked to anyone about his feelings for Doris; on this hot summer's afternoon he didn't intend to change that.

"Your problem, Daniel Archer, is that you think any sentence with more than half a dozen words in it is a long story. You ought to talk more . . . share your worries more. Why not try it sometimes?"

"Aye, maybe I will . . . one day."

"Why not now? It's a long, long time since I've had a decent conversation . . . not since your father died."

It was the first time Daniel had ever heard his mother use ordinary, plain language about his father's death. The memory was usually too painful and she always talked about him as having "met his Maker" or having "passed on". Maybe now really was the time for mother and son to talk. In any case, he wanted to ask Phoebe her views about getting a man in so that she could take it a bit easier.

"Why don't we go for a walk?"

His mother looked at him in surprise. Then, shaking her head, she laughed happily.

"You know, Daniel, I can't remember the last time I went for a walk. It must have been nearly twenty years ago, when you were still a tiny lad."

"Aye, well, I'll go slowly so that I don't tire you out!"

"Don't be cheeky! You're still my son and that means you're still liable to get a clip around the ear!"

Daniel was delighted to hear his mother in such good spirits, and he strode purposefully across the yard whistling for the dogs, Gypsy and Rover. They came bounding out of the kitchen and barked furiously before coming to heel.

"Right then, let's go. We'll take the Lakey Hill route, shall we?"

"Hey, wait a minute. I haven't got the right boots on. Let me go and change. I won't be long."

She hurried into the farmhouse. Daniel and the dogs waited for her by the path that would take them down past Hollowtree Farm and across the River Am to Lakey Hill. His mother was out again very quickly. As the sun caught her hair, the greyness disappeared and she suddenly looked like a sprightly young girl.

With the two dogs circling ahead of them they walked across the fields and clambered over the stile that took them through Hollowtree Farm and down into the village. It was tea-time and the green was deserted. They didn't see anyone except Percy Hood, who waved to them through the window of his new bakery shop. The window of the village stores next door was covered in posters advertising every kind of activity for miles around. Nancy Sawyer, who ran the shop and the post office, liked to think the world revolved around her, and she was always keen to pass on every scrap of information . . . and a fair bit of local gossip!

At the other end of the narrow main street they passed the village pond and forked to the right. They climbed over another stile and, with Gypsy and Rover scampering on ahead, made their way up the long, gentle slope of Lakey Hill. By the time they got to the top, Phoebe was slightly out of breath.

"Let's sit down for a while and admire the view."

"Aye, it's grand the way you can see the whole

village from here. I think that's why I like the walk so much."

Looking down on the cluster of houses and shops around the village green they could see smoke begin to drift up from the chimney of the Cat and Fiddle. The landlord, Sammy Plant, didn't usually light a fire in the summer, but he made an exception when there was a darts match on. That meant it would probably be nice and quiet in The Bull that evening.

Over to the left, beyond Marney's Farm, they could see Ambridge Hall, where a gardener was busy at work trimming the huge lawn. Brookfield lay slightly to the right of the Hall, and the farmhouse that they always thought of as being fairly big looked positively tiny by comparison with its neighbour.

To the right, looking across Meadow Farm towards Borchester, the Manor House came into view; there, too, a gardener marched ant-like backwards and forwards across the neat green lawn in front of the house.

Up here, the birdsong was so loud that it drowned any sounds that might otherwise have drifted up from the village.

"I can't think whatever made our Ben and Frank want to move away from all this. Can you, Daniel?"

Daniel looked carefully at his mother. She didn't seem to be unhappy or far away as she usually was when talking about the boys.

"You know why Frank went to New Zealand, Mother. He didn't want to join the army."

"Yes, but he didn't have to leave Ambridge. He could have stayed here. There were lots of other men who didn't go off to fight, and none of them went away from the village."

"Frank was different. He didn't want to kill anyone because of his principles. He was a pacifist and didn't want you and Dad to be affected by what he believed. He didn't want people to gossip about him being a coward because he knew how much it would upset you."

68

"Your dad and I could have put up with that easily enough. We knew he wasn't a coward."

Daniel wondered how you convince a whole village of something like that.

"It wasn't just that. Frank would always have been different. He couldn't fit in to a small place like Ambridge, where he would always be asked about why he didn't join up. He'd have been challenged all the time, and he didn't want that. He didn't want to have to explain all the time. He just asked to be left alone to lead his own life the way he wanted."

Phoebe looked at her eldest son. In a few simple words he had helped her to understand young Frank's problems, and she was grateful. Could he help explain Ben's sudden flight?

"Tell me about Ben."

"Ben?"

"Yes, Daniel. It's time you and I talked about him. Neither of us have been right since he left."

"You know we had a terrible fight?"

"Yes, of course I knew. How could I not, with all those terrible bruises and your split lip? But I never knew what it was about. I thought it must have been about Doris Forrest."

"It was partly about Doris, but it was mainly about Ben and the war and me and Brookfield."

"I don't understand."

Having just gone over much of it in his own head, it was easier for Daniel to explain.

"He was very unhappy when he came back from Flanders. He had been through terrible experiences there and I never gave him a chance to get them out of his system. You see, because I'd been in the army and because I'd been to France, I reckoned I knew as much about the war as anyone. I didn't . . . not Ben's kind of war. What he and his battalion went through was hell. It was a miracle that anyone lived through it."

"But how do you know all that if you never talked about it?"

"I got it from Percy Hood. He served alongside Ben all the way through Flanders. He told me about some of the terrible things that happened to them. Did you know that Ben saved Godfrey Winstanley's life by killing a German with his trench shovel?"

Mrs Archer was too shocked to answer. Like most people in the country, she knew very little about what had happened in the war, and certainly none of the details.

"Our Ben did that?"

"Yes . . . and if he hadn't, Godfrey Winstanley would have been just another name on the war memorial."

From where they sat they could see the memorial on the village green . . . a grey finger of stone that had become the new focal point of the village since Godfrey Winstanley had unveiled it earlier in the year. As they looked down on it, both reflected how lucky they were that the name Archer wasn't on the plaque. It was Phoebe who broke the silence.

"Ben never said anything about that. I never knew how brave he had been."

"Aye, he was brave, all right. When Percy was wounded, it was our Ben who carried him all the way from the front line to the field hospital because it was too dangerous for the stretcher-bearers. Carried him back through a shell bombardment . . . probably saved his life, too."

"Do you think if he had talked about it, things would have been better for him?"

"I'm not sure. He was very bitter and angry that everyone seemed to take all that the army did very much for granted. He felt the whole war was an awful, pointless waste of time."

Mrs Archer couldn't take it all in. She couldn't begin to understand the torment that her son had been through. She moved on to safer ground.

"You said you and Ben argued about Brookfield?"

"Yes . . . at least, at the time I thought it was about the farm. Looking back, it could be that he was fighting the war all over again."

Daniel flinched as he remembered the first crunching blow to his face, and he could almost taste the blood in his mouth.

"He was very mixed up. He said it was unfair that I'd been given the tenancy. I could understand that, but then he rambled on about me and the politicians conspiring to stop him being a farmer. That didn't make any kind of sense to me and I got very angry, I'm afraid, because he said I would have been happier if he'd never come back from the war. That was just rubbish, of course, but he wouldn't believe me and insisted that there wasn't room at Brookfield for the two of us."

"But if your father had still been alive, I'm sure there'd have been plenty of work for all three of you."

"Aye, that's probably right, but then he and I would have worked alongside each other as equals. With the tenancy going into my name, it was different for Ben. He would always have thought he was only working for me."

"What about Doris Forrest?"

"Oh, I think Doris is the one person who might have helped him to settle down in Ambridge . . . not that I knew that at the time, of course. I thought he had only a passing fancy for her. Again, you see, I was too wrapped up in myself to realise what was going on in his mind."

"You know I've always thought that it would be you that would wed Doris?"

Halfway down the hill, Gypsy and Rover were barking playfully at the tall figure of the young squire as he walked up towards them.

"Time we were getting back, Mother."

Phoebe looked at her son. She'd get no further with him today on the question of a wife.

CHAPTER EIGHT

Phoebe Archer looked at herself in the mirror for the fourth time. She was wearing a white lace-fronted blouse with a high collar, and she nervously fingered the heavy gilt brooch she'd pinned at her throat. She wasn't quite sure if it looked all right there. A thin wisp of greying hair escaped from the long pin that was supposed to be keeping it in place. With a sigh she hurriedly set about repairing the damage. As she checked the mirror yet again she saw that her face was drawn in an anxious look and she did her best to smile.

It was very silly worrying about what Mrs Lawson-Hope would think of her appearance. Sunday afternoon tea couldn't be the most formal of occasions, even at the Manor House. Still, Phoebe did want to look her best because it would be the first time in ages that she had been anywhere special.

She'd never been a great one for company when her husband was still alive, and since he had died more than two years earlier she seldom went out at all. Always busy around the farm, she hardly left it except for regular attendance at St Stephen's, where she managed to keep up with most of the village gossip. That was her choice, of course. Daniel was always going on at her to take life easier. He had recently started dropping hints about hiring a regular labourer, too.

It was Daniel who had insisted that she accept Mrs Lawson-Hope's invitation. She had been very surprised to receive the handwritten note in the first place, and the thought of visiting the big house so filled her with awe that her immediate reaction had been to concoct an excuse for not going. Daniel pointed out, however, that the invitation was for any Sunday afternoon. She couldn't possibly say there was never a day when she could get away from the farm without sounding very rude or giving everyone the impression that he was something of a slave-driver! Although he didn't actually say so, Phoebe had got the impression that he was less than anxious to cause any offence to the squire.

Phoebe took a last look in the mirror, smoothed down her skirt and carefully fixed her prettiest shawl around her shoulders. With the fields still warmed by the late summer sun, she didn't really need the shawl, but it was one that John had bought her during one of their rare shopping trips to Borchester, and it always made her feel quite dressy.

When she eventually went downstairs, Daniel was sitting at the kitchen table reading an old farming magazine and drinking a cup of tea.

"Ah, you're ready at long last. I was beginning to think you'd changed your mind again."

"I haven't been that long!"

"No, of course you haven't. I was only joking."

It was a long time since Daniel had seen his mother dressed up – so long, in fact, that he couldn't remember the last occasion. She always looked neat and smart when she went to church, of course, but this was different.

"You look very nice."

She smiled shyly and blushed, almost like a young girl.

"Do you really think so?"

"You look smashing. Now, come on, I've got the horse in harness already and she's probably champing at the bit."

Outside in the yard Daniel climbed up first onto the high seat of the wagon, and then offered his mother a hand up. When she was settled alongside him and had reassured herself that her hairstyle hadn't been damaged by her efforts, Daniel shook the reins and clicked his tongue to encourage the old mare to get going.

"Right, madam, the Manor House it is!"

As they clip-clopped slowly along the lane bounded by high hedges and grass verges covered in late summer flowers, Phoebe began to feel nervous again. She'd

73

never been a guest at the big house before, and she didn't know what to expect. Like all the other villagers, she had been to dozens of garden fetes there and had taken the opportunity to peep inside the house and see the grandness of it all. Once, she remembered having a cup of tea with Mrs Cooper, the housekeeper, but that was down in the kitchen. What would it be like above stairs? Hopefully one or two other local women would be there to save her having to talk just to Mrs Lawson-Hope and her posh, well-off friends.

"She won't bite you, you know."

Daniel had noticed the look of apprehension on his mother's face.

"I only hope Lisa Forrest or someone like that will be there. I won't know what to talk about otherwise."

"I doubt if you'll see Mrs Forrest there. Don't forget Doris is the lady's maid to Mrs Lawson-Hope, and it'd never do to be entertaining a servant's mother. There'll probably be lots of other folk there that you know."

All the way through the village, Phoebe kept hoping to see someone else going in the same direction, but now they were approaching the long drive up to the Manor House and there were still no signs of other visitors.

"Drop me off at the gate, please, Daniel."

"Don't be daft, Mother. The drive's half a mile long. I'll take you right up to the door. That's how invited guests should arrive, you know."

"No, Daniel. I'd rather clamber down from the wagon without being watched by the whole staff, if you don't mind."

Daniel laughed and reined in the horse. There was no point arguing.

"What about coming home? Do you want me to wait for you down here again?"

"I don't want you to wait anywhere, thank you. I haven't the faintest idea how long I'll be. I'll walk home when I've been dismissed!"

As the cart drove away Phoebe gave a little shiver of nervousness and pulled her shawl more tightly around

74

her shoulders for security. As she walked up the drive, now looking longer than ever, the gardener's lad was sweeping up the first fall of leaves with an old rake.

"Afternoon, missus."

"Afternoon."

She wasn't sure whether or not to say anything else. She didn't know if the boy recognised her or was perhaps just being polite because he thought she was someone important. She blushed at her own awkwardness and hurried on towards the house.

As she crossed the last few yards of the drive she noticed that it wasn't pitted and rutted like the track at home, nor were there any weeds growing through the carefully raked shale. The brasswork on the huge door was gleaming so brightly that it seemed a shame to put fingermarks on the bell-pull. The maid obviously thought the same thing, probably because she had to clean it, and the door was opened almost as soon as Phoebe's foot touched the top step.

"Afternoon, Mrs Archer."

It was young Lisa Scroby, looking very pretty in a neat black dress with a white apron and fancy little white cap.

"Mrs Lawson-Hope is expecting you and I've to take you straight through to her sitting-room."

The slight air of reserve made it obvious that the girl either didn't want to talk or that she wasn't encouraged to have any kind of personal conversation with visitors. She ushered Phoebe across the hallway's highly polished floor, not giving her much chance to take a proper look at the beautiful paintings on the walls or at the furniture. Almost timidly, Lisa tapped on the sitting-room door.

"Come in!"

As Lisa opened the door and showed her in, Phoebe was horrified to see that Mrs Lawson-Hope was sitting by herself in the huge room. No one else had arrived yet. She was too early, and someone had once told her that that was a breach of etiquette.

Mrs Lawson-Hope rose and came to greet her.

"Ah, Mrs Archer, how nice to see you. Do come and sit down."

"I'm sorry I'm so early."

"Early? No, no, you're exactly on time. Lisa, will you tell Mrs Cooper that my guest has arrived and we'll have tea just as soon as she can arrange it, please."

The maid dipped a little curtsy and left.

As Phoebe perched herself nervously on the edge of a chintz-covered armchair, she realised that no other guests were expected. Although she had known Lettie Lawson-Hope for more than twenty years, she had never really had a proper conversation with her. Usually, they exchanged pleasantries after church services and on the rare occasions when Mrs Lawson-Hope attended the Women's Institute meetings, but that was about all. Apart from being round about the same age, Phoebe would never have considered they had anything in common, their worlds seemed so far apart.

"I'm so pleased you were able to come. I know how busy you are up at Brookfield, and I thought it might be difficult for you to get away. It's good of you to take the trouble. I do appreciate it. I don't get the chance to see many people these days, and you and I seem to have so much in common that I thought it would be nice to have the chance to talk to each other."

Phoebe was saved from any immediate response by a knock on the door. Doris Forrest came in carrying a heavy tray. She smiled, but, like Lisa Scroby, offered no more personal greeting. As the cups and saucers were being set out on a very elegant side-table, Phoebe was able to have a look around the room, noticing with a housewife's eye how exquisitely it had been furnished. The chintz covering the chair on which she was sitting matched all the other chairs and sofas in the room, and the same material hung as curtains from both the tall windows. The walls were covered in heavy gilt framed paintings of flowers and vegetables, which

76

seemed a little odd to Phoebe. She would have expected family portraits or something of that sort. Who would want to look at flowers and vegetables all the time?

By now, her feelings of awe at her grand surroundings had diminished slightly, and she was able to look at the room more critically. The only problem with it, she thought, is that it just doesn't look lived in. Nothing appeared out of place, and the plump cushions on the chairs looked as though no one had ever sat on them.

"Would you like me to pour the tea, Mrs Lawson-Hope?"

"No, thank you, Doris. I'll do that. You can slip off now and have an hour or two to yourself."

Doris smiled gratefully and then she, too, gave a little curtsy before hurrying away.

"Doris is a very good girl, the best maid I've ever had. She's been a bit restless since her younger brother, Edward, died earlier in the year, and I think she may feel it's time to move on to something better. But she's been brave enough to ignore her own unhappiness and says she won't leave me until I've fully got over the colonel's death. I do appreciate that."

Phoebe was so wrapped up in her nervousness that she had almost forgotten that young Ted Forrest had been killed in a riding accident the previous January when he had gone out to follow the Borsetshire Hunt. His horse had refused at a five-bar gate and Ted had taken a very heavy tumble – he was dead by the time they got him to the hospital. It was only a week after his twentieth birthday, and the whole village had been devastated by the news. Lisa Forrest had been so distraught that she hadn't left the house for months. Even now she went out only to go to church. Some said that William Forrest would never get over the death of his elder son. The young man had already been set to follow in his footsteps as an assistant gamekeeper, and William had been very proud of him. The one blessing was that little Tommy, who was still only ten, was too young to really understand what had happened. Doris had cried a lot at the time, but she had gone back to work at the big house fairly quickly and that had probably taken her mind off the accident, though deep down she was still grieving for her brother.

"Of course, you know Doris quite well, don't you?"

"Yes, I do. I've known her mother all my life. We went to school together and I was her bridesmaid when she married William. In fact, don't tell her, but lots of the clothes that Doris wore as a baby were hand-me-downs from my sons!"

She could hardly believe that she had said anything so silly and boring, but Mrs Lawson-Hope laughed.

"It must be very nice to have friends like that with whom you can share things. When I had my children, I had nurses and nannies but, of course, they were never interested in me, only in the babies. I didn't have any friends around me because all my old school chums lived so far away and I didn't know anyone in Ambridge then."

Phoebe was almost shocked. She had never thought of the lady of the manor not having lots of friends. She had always assumed that life in the big house was one long social whirl, full of activity and excitement.

"I was saying a moment ago that you and I have so much in common, and I thought it might be nice for both of us if we compared notes, as it were?"

Phoebe felt she was on unsafe ground, but she had no intention of showing it. She had ignored the phrase earlier, but now if the squire's mother said they had a lot in common . . . well, then, they had a lot in common. Only it would have to be Mrs Lawson-Hope who pointed out the similarities. All she could see at the moment was the evidence of their differences.

Sipping tea from the delicate bone-china cup, she was all too well aware of the contrast in their ways of life. It's true that she had a very nice set of good-quality china herself, but it was one that she'd inherited from her mother and she wasn't quite sure how many pieces were left. Several cups and saucers had been broken by the calloused fingers of the hard-working farmers who were the only visitors to Brookfield. In any case, those that were left certainly didn't match up to the dainty, fragile quality of Mrs Lawson-Hope's china, and she could hardly imagine her having to worry much about replacements for any breakages. The housekeeper or someone would, no doubt, do that without even having to be told.

There was another knock at the door, louder this time, and Lisa Scroby came in looking quite flustered.

"I'm very sorry to intrude, ma'am, but Mrs Cooper is having some problems in the kitchen. She wonders if you could possibly spare her a few minutes."

"Certainly not. She knows I have a guest. Tell her that whatever it is will have to wait."

"Begging your pardon, ma'am, but she did say it was most urgent."

The look of agitation on the young girl's face obviously communicated itself to Mrs Lawson-Hope.

"Oh, very well. I'm terribly sorry, Mrs Archer. Will you forgive me if I leave you alone for a few moments?"

"Yes, of course. Please don't worry about me."

The interruption came almost as a relief for Phoebe, and she welcomed the chance to relax, and to take a more leisurely look around the room. For all its elegance and finery, all the pictures on the walls and the highly polished furniture, she still felt she wouldn't change places with Mrs Lawson-Hope. She would never feel at home anywhere but at Brookfield Farm.

"I'm sorry about that, Mrs Archer. We're having quite a few problems downstairs at the moment."

Mrs Lawson-Hope had come back into the room, looking far from her usual composed self.

"George doesn't really concern himself with the household. He says he has enough problems running the estate. That means I have to instruct the butler, who, as you can imagine, doesn't take very kindly to taking his orders from a mere woman. He and Mrs Cooper have been having another row and it was threatening to disrupt this evening's supper arrangement. I do wish George would sort it out, but I'm sure if I left it to him we wouldn't have any servants at all."

Phoebe smiled. She'd heard that the young squire was being very unsquirelike around the village. Walter Gabriel said he had dropped in on them one morning and had got quite upset when Annie had curtsied and Walter had called him "sir". Apparently, he had said he wanted to treat everyone as equals, but that didn't go down too well with the villagers. They were happy with the way things had been in the old squire's day and weren't looking for any changes.

It seemed as if young George Lawson-Hope's progressive ideas were not only being misunderstood in the village, but were causing problems at the Manor House as well. Phoebe felt quite sorry for him because he seemed such a nice young man.

"George is so different from his father. He wants to do everything his own way and doesn't seem to be prepared to learn anything from the way things have been done in the past."

Phoebe heard an echo of her own comments about young Daniel's way of going on just after he had come back from the army to take over at Brookfield.

"You know, Mrs Lawson-Hope, you can't really expect the boy simply to follow in his father's footsteps. Do you do things the way your mother did? I know I don't."

"I suppose you're right."

Phoebe hadn't expected quite such ready agreement from her hostess. Having worked up the courage to offer an opinion, she pressed on with what she had to say.

"When I lost my husband and Daniel started running the farm, I kept comparing everything he did with how my John would have done it. I used to get quite upset.

80

Sometimes I thought it was an insult to John that Daniel should change anything, and I'm sure I must have nagged the poor lad half to death. I honestly don't know how he managed to put up with me going on at him so much."

"That's exactly how I find myself responding to George! His father was such a fine man, but George says he was much too authoritarian. He says you can't direct people in the same way in this day and age. You've got to let people take more responsibility for their own destiny. I don't really understand, and I doubt if Colonel Lawson-Hope would if he were still alive."

Phoebe could recognise the sadness in Mrs Lawson-Hope's eyes as she talked about her husband. She had never really known the colonel, but John had always spoken of him with great respect, and everyone in the village had certainly admired his courage during the last painful months of his life when he had come back from the war. The gas damage to his lungs had given him a terrible gauntness and he had had to lean very heavily on a walking-stick. He should have been in a bathchair, but his pride wouldn't allow that.

Towards the end it was obvious to everyone that he was beginning to lose control of the estate's business and couldn't really keep track of all that was going on over several thousand acres and more than a dozen farms and smallholdings. At the same time everyone felt very sorry for young George. As the youngest son, he hadn't been trained to manage the estate, and would never have been expected to take it on if both his elder brothers, Cedric and Hugh, hadn't been killed in the war.

"I don't think you can expect George to be anything but his own man. He can't be his father. For a start, he doesn't have his father's experience."

"I think I believe that, and I think I believe in what George is trying to do, but I worry what other people think. I desperately don't want them to feel he's shrinking from his responsibilities."

It was clear that Mrs Lawson-Hope was still the squire's lady and still very concerned with appearances, but

Phoebe wasn't too sure that she wasn't right about the villagers. They really did like to know where they stood with their landlord. They actually needed somebody like the squire to look up to.

Maybe that was a problem the young squire and her own Daniel shared: neither of them had a father to look up to or to turn to for advice.

"Perhaps it will be different when they get married?"

Phoebe was almost surprised that she had spoken her thoughts out loud.

"They?"

"I'm sorry, I was thinking about my Daniel, too. I don't think mothers are very good substitutes for fathers. I try to help as much as I can, but I know Daniel sometimes gets embarrassed that people will think he's tied to my apron strings."

"You're probably right but, you know, I can't see George taking a wife and settling down for a while yet. He's positively unfriendly to most of the young girls he meets at our social occasions. The only girl he shows any interest in is young Doris."

"Doris Forrest? Your maid?"

"Yes. He says he likes talking to her because she's got a lovely sense of humour and much more conversation than the type of girl he usually has to escort to the hunt ball and other functions."

Even Phoebe could see the difficulty in that. William Forrest would be outraged at the thought of his daughter's name being linked with the squire's in any personal way. There were too many folk tales handed down from the past about how the gentry of bygone days had treated servant girls for any father to be happy with that kind of situation. Remembering her own son's past interest in Doris, Phoebe imagined that Daniel would be equally shocked at any such suggestion.

"They're not actually walking out, are they?"

"Good heavens, no. That would be unthinkable! My son and my lady's maid? I hope you didn't think I was

82

suggesting anything like that. I was just explaining his lack of interest in suitable girls."

In other circumstances Phoebe might have felt hurt or angry by such a sharp response, but she was too busy feeling relieved for her friends William and Lisa Forrest and for Daniel.

Mrs Lawson-Hope must have realised she had sounded very dismissive of her young maid.

"I'm sorry. I didn't mean that the way it must have sounded."

"It's quite all right, Mrs Lawson-Hope. I understand. I'm just as anxious that my son should marry the right girl."

Her hostess was clearly relieved at Phoebe's words and quickly jumped at the chance to move the conversation away from her own son.

"Do you think Daniel will marry soon?"

"Well, I'm pretty sure he'd like to."

It was nearly two years since Daniel had been on the verge of proposing to Doris Forrest, but her recent conversation with him on Lakey Hill had told her that he quite often thought about taking a wife still.

"His problem is that he's much too shy. He doesn't have any girlfriends and I don't know how that will change. He works very hard on the farm and seldom goes anywhere other than The Bull. I can't imagine him meeting the right girl there, can you?"

Mrs Lawson-Hope had never been in the local pub and had no idea what kind of people went there. She didn't really want to know.

"How old is Daniel now?"

"He'll be twenty-four in October."

"Oh, he's a year older than George. So if he's not marrying for a while, it's quite likely that George won't have thought too much about it either. That means I needn't start making my plans to move into the Dower House quite yet!"

Phoebe smiled. Mrs Lawson-Hope didn't realise how lucky she was having the luxury of another house to live in with plenty of rooms for servants and as much privacy as she wanted. When her Daniel married, the best she could hope for would be that his wife would be happy for her to stay on at Brookfield.

Whatever Mrs Lawson-Hope might think they had in common, there were certainly considerable differences, too.

CHAPTER NINE

The sweat glistened on Daniel's brow as he swung the heavy wooden shaft of the plough around at the end of another impeccably straight furrow. As the pair of horses pressed forward again at his command he kept a firm grip on the thick handles of the plough, enjoying the sensation of the sharp blades ripping through the firm clay and turning over the sods.

It was a bright October afternoon, and with the warmth of the sun on his back Daniel felt that it was great to be alive. Dozens of wagtails wheeled around in the air, following the plough in search of worms. At the far end of the half-acre field, a large crowd of spectators cheered him on. He was the last of the contestants in Ambridge's annual ploughing match. He knew exactly what he had to do to win.

Most of the day he had watched in admiration as his friends and neighbours, as well as ploughmen from all around the district, had tested their skills behind the plough. The standards this year were higher than ever. Halfway through his stint Daniel was definitely up with the leaders. The man to beat was George Grundy, who, despite regular visits to the ale tent, had kept his plough straight and true and still managed to finish in record time. Now, with yet another flagon of ale in his fist, he was clearly beginning to celebrate his victory without waiting to see how Daniel would fare.

"Might as well give me the trophy right away, Squire. I don't reckon Dan Archer will finish afore the night's gone. He's no match for the likes of me!"

A tall, commanding figure in a shirt that was open to the waist, George Grundy was telling anybody who would listen how easy it had been.

"It was no bother holding straight. Shortest five-mile plough I've ever done. Just like a Sunday afternoon stroll. I could do it all over again right now."

He crowed with laughter and waved his pot of ale in the air, spilling it over several other spectators. Some of his cronies, keeping up with him pint for pint, roared their approval and urged the young squire to declare their man the winner without any further ceremony. Daniel's supporters became just as noisy in demanding that he be given a fair chance like everyone else, and the excitement mounted as the competition moved towards its climax.

Although enjoying the general atmosphere, George Lawson-Hope urged everyone to be patient and wait until the contest was finished. His suggestion was met by a barrage of good-natured catcalls from the Grundy camp and whoops of approval from the Archer fans.

Ignoring all the distractions, Daniel urged his horses on faster. Prince and Bessie were two of the best beasts in Ambridge and he was very proud of his ploughing skills. He didn't want to be beaten by someone like George who, rightly or wrongly, had the reputation of being one of the worst farmers in the county. It wasn't so much that he wasn't capable of running the farm, it was just that he preferred to pass his time playing cricket. He spent more of the summer months in white flannels than ever he did in working clothes. Even today he had simply tied up his corduroy trousers with a couple of strings at the knees to keep the bottoms out of the mud. Mind you, George had at least ten more years' experience than Daniel, and whatever anyone else might say he had made a beautiful job of his half-acre.

"Come on, Daniel, only a few more lengths to go! You can do it, me old pal, me old beauty!"

Above the general noise, Daniel heard Walter Gabriel urging him on.

"He's going to need more than encouragement from you, young Walter. It's the Archangel Gabriel he needs on his side if he's to win today!"

George Grundy roared at his own joke and his mates cheered in half-drunken approval.

"Don't you underestimate Daniel Archer. He's a good 'un. He'll give you a run for your money any day, you'll see!"

"I'll tell you this, Walter Gabriel – there's nothing you can tell me about Dan Archer. I was his sergeant major in the army, and I gave him many a roasting when we were in France together. I reckon I'm going to dish out another one today."

"Just wait and see, just wait and see, that's all. Don't you go counting no chickens yet. Daniel Archer is as strong as an ox, and he's one of the best farmers in this district despite just being a slip of a lad like me."

Walter jumped about from foot to foot and yelled more encouragement in his pal's direction.

"How would you know about farming, Walter Gabriel? You're hardly old enough to be out of nappies, and that strip of land you've got can hardly even be described as a smallholding. How come you think you can judge who's a good farmer? Anyway, there's a difference between milking a few cows and ploughing a half-acre field!"

Before Walter could get into the argument, a great groan went up from the crowd and he knew that Daniel had made a mistake. Bessie, the left-hand horse, had missed her footing on a turn, and Daniel had been unable to hold the weight of the plough or stop it lurching off course. The kink in the furrow stood out like a sore thumb. No one needed to wait for the judges' assessment. Daniel had lost valuable points and had no chance of winning.

At that point most men would have given up and beaten a hasty retreat to the ale tent, but not Daniel. He still had a few furrows to go, and he spat on his hands to ease the blisters and urged the horses on again to the sympathetic cheers of Walter and his other friends.

His determination paid off and he finished to a well-earned round of applause, with even George Grundy joining in.

"Bad luck, Dan. It's not as easy as it looks when an expert does it!"

"There's no need to be cocky, George. You won fair and square, so why not just enjoy your victory?"

Daniel's feet were hot and painful and the skin had started to peel from his blistered hands. Perhaps he wouldn't have noticed any of these things if he had won, but as it was he felt pretty miserable and didn't relish having his nose rubbed in the dirt as well.

"What about having a go at showing us how it should be done, Squire?"

George Grundy turned his attention to young George Lawson-Hope, who looked distinctly uneasy.

"Your old man could hold a plough straight with the best of us."

The young squire was sick of hearing exaggerated tales about his father's ability. He had loved his father and admired him very much, but he felt himself being constantly compared with him, and it was becoming very wearing. For several weeks before the ploughing match the villagers had begged him to act as a judge . . . just as his father had always done. He'd refused, saying that he wasn't enough of an expert to make a proper assessment of the men's efforts and that wouldn't be fair to them. In the end they had reluctantly accepted that three local farmers should act in his stead.

All the same, he had readily agreed to attend the match and present the prizes, and had even donated a couple of barrels of ale. Yet ever since he had arrived at nine o'clock in the morning he had felt himself the subject of some disapproval. Because he wasn't doing what his father had done, many of the villagers appeared to think he was letting them down. Now he was being got at for not being a jolly ploughboy!

"The year afore last, your dad was particularly scathing about the way some of us managed our half-acres, and I remember someone telling him that if he felt so blessed clever, he ought to have a go himself."

"It sounds very much as if that someone could have been you, Mr Grundy."

"No, it wasn't me. I don't remember who it was, but the thing is that the old squire took off his jacket, rolled up his sleeves and ended up ploughing half a dozen furrows as straight as any man in the competition!"

"Well, I'm sorry to disappoint you, but I'm more than ready to admit that I'm no match for any of you when it comes to ploughing."

Buoyed up with drink and his success, George Grundy was determined to harass the young man.

"How about judging the mangolds and swedes, then, Squire? Think you're up to that?"

To make a day of the ploughing match, another tent was always set up for the womenfolk to display prize specimens from their vegetable gardens; the judging was usually done by the squire's wife. This year it had been done by George's mother. The insult hit home, but the squire decided to bite his tongue. He had been taught never to be rude to his elders.

"I think we ought to get on with the presentation of the prizes so that you can get back to the ale tent, Mr Grundy."

Seeing that there was little sport to be had at the squire's expense, George Grundy accepted the winner's trophy and marched off unsteadily at the head of his small band of supporters in search of more beer.

Daniel had overcome his disappointment at not winning the competition and in his usual generous way came up to congratulate the winner, only to have his proffered hand ignored.

"I'm sorry about that, Squire. George can be an awkward beggar when he feels like it."

"No, no. There's no apology necessary. In a way Grundy's right. If I'm to be accepted as the squire, I ought to be able to give the people the kind of leadership they want. That's the law of the countryside. I know my father would have been able to set an example, but the truth is I'm not even sure that I want to. I don't see why people should look to me for guidance on how to run their lives just because I own a piece of land."

"It's a bit more than a piece of land, Squire! It's nearly half the district, and includes most of the farms around Ambridge."

The young man looked suddenly tired.

"Please don't remind me, Daniel. I feel enough responsibility already. I'm not quite twenty-three yet and I feel that I have no life beyond managing the estate. Don't you sometimes feel the same? I mean, you're in very much the same boat as me, having to take things over unexpectedly."

"I think there's a fair bit of difference between taking over the tenancy of Brookfield Farm and becoming the squire of the whole village."

"Yes, I suppose you're right, and you're also lucky in that you'd had some experience on the farm before your father died, and you'd seen a bit of life in the army."

The noise from the ale tent was getting louder, and they could hear George Grundy's gang launch into a chorus of bawdy songs.

"I say, Daniel, do you have to stay here much longer?"

"No, not really. Why?"

"Well . . . I was wondering if you might agree to you and I disappearing and having a quiet chat somewhere else. I'm afraid I'm not awfully good at the bonhomie bit, and I suspect that I might forget my manners and get quite rude if that Grundy fellow starts on me again."

"Aye, right you are, then, but I'll have to say cheerio to one or two friends first."

Daniel went off to find Walter Gabriel, who was more than holding his own, both in the volume of beer he was drinking and in the volume of noise he was making.

"You had bad luck there, Daniel, me old pal, me old beauty. I was just saying to these good people that if your horse hadn't slipped at the crucial moment you'd be the one supping your ale out of the victor's cup instead of that braggart, George Grundy."

"Not so loud, Walter. We don't want to start any more argument at this stage. I'm just off now. I only came to say cheerio and to thank you for your support."

"Oh, come on, Daniel. There's still a lot of ale to be drunk. You don't have to go home yet. You don't have a wife waiting to nag you to death if you're five minutes later than expected. Why are you rushing off?"

"I'm not rushing off. I'm just going, that's all. In any case, I'm sure you and that crowd will manage to empty the barrel without any assistance from me. I'll see you later in the week. Cheerio."

Daniel didn't wait for Walter to muster any further arguments but hurried out of the tent to find the squire. Although the nights were beginning to draw in, there was still an hour or so of sunlight to enjoy while all his aches and pains from the ploughing eased away.

"How about a stroll?"

"That's exactly what I had in mind, Daniel . . . do you mind my calling you Daniel, by the way, or should I call you Mr Archer?"

"Don't be daft, lad. You'd make me feel positively ancient if you did that. I'm not much older than you. It was my twenty-fourth birthday last week."

"I'm sorry. I didn't mean to imply that you were old or anything. It's just that you seem to have so much more experience than me."

"Let's not get it out of perspective, Squire. I only did some labouring around the farm before I went into the army. Buying hay from French farmers isn't exactly the best preparation for running a farm back here in England."

"All right . . . but before we go any further I insist that you must stop calling me 'Squire'. Let's just be George and Daniel, please."

Daniel smiled uncertainly. He liked George Lawson-Hope very much. Under other circumstances they might well have been as good pals as he was with Walter Gabriel. However, the squire was still the squire and Daniel still owed his livelihood to the young man. Nothing could change that.

"Aye . . . I'll gladly call you George, but you'll have to excuse me if the squire bit pops out every now and then. It's not easy to break the habit of a lifetime."

George grinned hugely. He felt he had won at least a small victory in his battle to change some of the old ways of the squirearchy.

"Can we walk back to Brookfield, Daniel? I'd love to have a look around your farm. Everyone says you've worked miracles on it over the last couple of years."

Strolling up through the village at the squire's side Daniel was glad that most of the other men were still back at the celebrations. He didn't want any of them to think that he was putting on airs and graces and becoming over-friendly with the gentry.

As they neared the farm they were greeted by the loud barking of Gypsy and Rover, and then Daniel's mother came out of the kitchen to see what had caused the noise. She looked flustered when she saw who was with Daniel.

"Good afternoon, Squire. Is there something wrong, Daniel?"

"No, Mother, there's nothing wrong. The squire has just come to have a look around the farm, that's all."

"That's right, Mrs Archer. It was one of those spur-of-the-moment things. I hope it's not inconvenient. I could come back some other time."

"Oh no, it's not inconvenient at all. I'll go and put the kettle on for a cup of tea. I've got some freshly-baked cakes, too. It won't take a minute."

"That's very kind of you, Mrs Archer, but, honestly, I've just come to see the farm. I don't want to put you to any trouble."

Daniel added his reassurances and his mother eventually disappeared back into the kitchen, still looking very uncertain. He quietened the dogs and locked them in the barn.

"Right, George, let's get on. What would you like to see first?"

"Well, I notice you've got your dairy cattle inside already. Isn't it early for that?"

"Oh no. With all the recent rain we've been having the pasture has started getting very wet, and with such heavy soil in these parts the cows were beginning to cause a lot of damage with their hooves. If I hadn't moved them inside, they would have wrecked the whole field within a couple of days."

"How do you feed them? Isn't it twice as much work as leaving them to graze outside?"

"It's swings and roundabouts. Having them inside makes the milking an awful lot easier. I don't have to go out in the cold or the rain to bring them in at six o'clock in the morning before I can even start the milking, and I don't have to worry about them finding shelter from the winds. Feeding them can be a bit of a nuisance, but I promise you it's a small price to pay for all the other advantages."

"You must think I'm very silly asking such basic questions, but I really know very little about what goes on around the farms. You see, when I was growing up it was Cedric who was expected to inherit the estate. I never took much interest in it all. I wanted to go to university and study to become a doctor. The war came as a terrible shock, and when Cedric and Hugh didn't come back it was clear that I'd have to give up that idea because I'd have to take over here some day. Then, when my father died, it was all down to me and the 'some day' was suddenly today. I tell you, Daniel, just a year ago I could only just have told you the difference between a cow and a bull, and now I'm supposed to be responsible for all these thousands of acres and the livelihood of dozens of farmers like you."

Daniel felt sorry for his companion, yet there was little he could do to help. George Lawson-Hope had inherited enormous responsibilities, and he'd have to cope with them himself unless he was to see the estate being broken up.

"Don't worry, George, you're learning the best way . . . by actually doing the job. You can't read books about living in the countryside or about understanding the seasons and the weather or about why some crops will grow in one field but not in the next one. It all comes with experience. At least, that's what my father told me, and from the little I know already it's beginning to happen for me. You don't want to worry about asking silly questions. We all ask daft questions in our time. As Walter Gabriel keeps saying, we'd all look a lot dafter if we didn't ask questions and just pressed on thinking that we knew what we were doing!"

"All right then, Daniel. Let me ask another silly question. Why do we charge you a much lower rent for your acreage than we do most of the other tenants in the district?"

"Well, I suspect that's because Brookfield isn't exactly an ideal holding. It just happens that with the lie of the land, too many of our fields face north. Southern slopes are much more valuable because they tend to warm up that much more quickly, which means that crops start growing that much earlier."

George laughed and shook his head in disbelief.

"Is it really as simple as that? I've been puzzling over it for weeks and I couldn't think of any logical explanation. I would have asked the factor, but he already thinks I'm a blithering idiot and I really couldn't face any more of his scorn."

"It's worth remembering, George, that nearly everything in the countryside has a very simple solution."

"Is that really true, Daniel? If it is, why can't we find the way out of this wretched forelock-tugging business? Why can't we be equals? Why should all those tenants have to defer to me and call me squire or sir? Do you know, I'm sure half of them don't even know what my Christian name is."

"It's a great pity my brother Ben isn't around. You and he could have a fascinating conversation. He became a socialist after the war and he was convinced that Ramsay MacDonald and his party were going to make everybody equal. You sound just like him. Maybe you could become Borsetshire's first socialist squire? Maybe you could stand for parliament?"

"I don't think I ever met Ben. I know there was great excitement when he came back from the war, but I was up in London with some relatives at the time while Mother was trying to get over the shock of Cedric and Hugh being killed. What sort of chap is he? Do you ever hear from him?"

"He's in Canada now. We hear from him very occasionally, but then he never was a great letter-writer. I remember my mother complaining that she only ever got one proper letter from him during the whole war. All she usually received from him were those awful field-postcard things."

George Lawson-Hope looked at Daniel, obviously uncertain as to whether or not to ask his next question.

"You were in the war, weren't you, Daniel? In my father's regiment? He would never talk about his experience, and I could never understand why. Do you mind if I ask what it was like?"

"I was in the regiment, yes. I never saw the war, though. I was with your father in France waiting to go up the Line when I got word that I had to come back to Ambridge because Dad had died. I spent my time in what my brother once described as a very cushy billet."

"At least you were in the army. That's more than I can claim. I was too damned young."

"It's a pity your father didn't tell you more about his experiences, because you might not have been so frustrated at being left behind. He and my brother were both at Passchendaele and by all accounts that was one of the most hellish battles of the war. Thousands of men were killed and many more – like your father – injured so badly that they were virtually

95

finished for life. That's why so many hospitals have had to be opened for disabled ex-servicemen. You should be glad to have missed all that. I certainly am."

"Perhaps you're right, Daniel. Maybe there isn't anything heroic about dying in action."

"You and I have to forget all about that now, George. It's the likes of you and me who have to pick up where those lads left off. We have to do our bit for the country now so that their sacrifice won't have been wasted."

CHAPTER TEN

If a prize had been going for musical energy, it would have been won hands down by the Borchester Town Silver Band. Resplendent in navy blue uniforms, with white caps over red faces, the bandsmen – aged from eight to eighty – looked as if they were trying to blow their own heads off, and the sound of their music could be heard all over the Vale of Am. Anything missing by way of tunefulness was made up for in volume.

For as long as anyone could remember the band had been the centrepiece of the Ambridge summer fete. The villagers considered themselves honoured that the famous band should make the long drive from Borchester each year just to play for them.

The villagers weren't to know that they were the long-term beneficiaries of a certain amount of bribery that had ensured that each ride was softened by an unspecified number of beer flagons, so that the visit had become one of the highlights of the bandsmen's calendar. The old squire of Ambridge had had the reputation of being the best host in the county; his hospitality was the talk at rehearsals throughout the year. His son, George, was no less generous.

The village fete was held every year on the second Saturday of July on the Manor House lawn – July being chosen because it offered the best chance of decent weather but also because it was one of the quieter months in the farming calendar. With luck, the hay would have been safely gathered in and the corn harvest wouldn't have started. Even the dairy farmers had it a little bit easier then, because the cows were beginning to dry out for the autumn calving and that meant less milking had to be done.

Preparations for the fete began much earlier in the year, almost as soon as the annual pantomime was over. Nearly everyone in the village was roped in to help in some way. Even the most truculent farmers were persuaded to do their bit, and this year the organising committee – under the chairmanship of Mrs Lawson-Hope – had been amazed at the readiness of George Grundy to supply the bales of straw that were used as makeshift seats.

The scene on the broad lawns of the Manor House was one of bustling gaiety. For once no one seemed to mind the grey skies.

The band was playing on a shaky-looking stage devised by Walter Gabriel out of an old hay trolley that had lost its wheels. He had attached four long poles to it, over which he had stretched a rumpled tarpaulin, and he'd painted the whole thing a bright blue. He'd then persuaded his long-suffering wife Annie to decorate it in red and white crepe paper. For most of the morning both of them had been sitting in front of the stage admiring their handiwork, mindless of the crashing sounds around them.

The squire's staff had erected a marquee, topped off by bunting that fluttered in the gentle breeze. Inside, the committee ladies had provided an amazing array of food – freshly-cut sandwiches, home-made pies, newly baked cakes, jellies, trifles and huge bowls of big fat strawberries that had been picked just after dawn.

At the risk of incurring his mother's displeasure, the squire had commandeered the pony-rides concession for himself and was cheerfully leading a hollow-backed beast across the lawn at a trot while three youngsters clung on for dear life and squealed with a mixture of pleasure and fear. The pony, its hooves swathed in specially knitted socks to prevent damage to the soft turf, was glistening with sweat and one of the stable lads stood by with a bucket of water to give it a quick swill down between customers. George Lawson-Hope looked as if he could do with the same treatment!

His butler, Mr Webber – no one knew his Christian name, although he had worked for the family for nearly thirty years – looked on with grave disapproval from his vantage point at the coconut shy, where he was acting as custodian of the small wooden balls that he handed out three at a time in return for a penny. On rare occasions he had been known to let some customers have a free throw, and Tilly Sawyer, one of the scullery maids, was flirting with him to see if it would work for her. Just as she was about to give up, his stern face cracked in the briefest of smiles, and with an almost ludicrous wink he handed her the balls.

"Roll up, roll up. Three balls for a penny. Come and have a go at winning a coconut!"

In this one brief burst of uninhibited exhibitionism, the butler exhausted his good nature for the year. Tilly Sawyer would no doubt pay dearly for her flightiness later.

At the improvised skittle alley, George Grundy and Percy Hood were arguing over whose turn it was to hurl the heavy wooden balls at the ninepins.

"Come on, George, you've already had three goes."

"So what? I can have as many goes as I want as long as I pay. There's no rule that says that I can't. Is there, Amos?"

Amos Perkins, who was unfortunate enough to be in charge of the skittles, grunted noncommittally. He didn't want to get involved in any unpleasantness.

"Why don't you go off and play your blessed cricket and let the rest of us try our hand?"

"You go and knead your dough, Percy Hood. I might just stay here for the rest of the day."

Percy, who had seen the initial exchanges as a bit of good-natured banter, recognised the edge in George Grundy's voice and whispered sharply in his ear.

"You watch it, George. I know you can't afford to squander your money. You owe me quite a few bob for your bread and cakes. If I was of a mind, I might just not let your missus have any more things on tick until you've settled your bill!"

George Grundy glowered and looked as if he were about to burst into a rage. Instead, he hurled his last ball at the skittles, missed by miles, and stormed off in the general direction of the beer. Amos Perkins laughed in relief.

"I reckon you deserve a free go for getting rid of that blighter, Percy. Be my guest."

A small knot of children was gathered over a bucket of water, taking it in turns to drop in a ha'penny in the hope of covering the shiny new sixpence that lay on the bottom. If you did, it was yours. The tanner bucket, as it was called, looked deceptively simple. The grown-ups had long since learned about the treachery of those few inches of water, but the youngsters were still convinced that they could work out at exactly which point their coin ought to hit the surface to fall to the bottom at the right spot.

"You've got to drop it in from the left."

"No . . . from the right."

"Try getting a bit closer to the bucket."

"You need to hit the water about an inch and a half away from the tanner."

"Drop it in edge-on."

"No . . . it's best if you let it go in flat."

The shrewder youngsters stood around watching everyone else's effort closely, calculating the possible angles of descent. Later in the day, Jesse Jordan, the long-time tanner bucket specialist, would frustrate them even further by putting a second sixpenny piece in the water.

When Daniel Archer arrived at the fete, he looked around with very little interest. He hadn't wanted to come at all because he reckoned he had better things to do around Brookfield, and he hated having to wear a suit, which was all but compulsory. However, his mother had been inveigled on to the committee by Mrs Lawson-Hope, and the least he could do to support her was to come to spend a few pence on some of the sideshows.

He toyed with the idea of entering the wood-chopping contest, but there was a long queue of sturdy teenagers already stripped to the waist and anxiously spitting on their hands as they waited to step up to the chopping block. He wasn't in the mood for hanging around.

"I'll come back later, Fred."

Fred Barratt grinned at him and nodded towards the boys.

"By the time this lot's finished, I reckon there won't be any wood left!"

As Daniel headed towards the darts stall his mother came out of the marquee. She was wearing a long flowing summer frock that would have looked prettier in the sunshine. She waved and came across to talk to him, almost having to shout to be heard above the noise from the band, which had struck up again with even greater gusto.

"Have you been here long, Daniel?"

"No, I've only just arrived. I wanted to do a bit of scything before I came out."

"Ah well, better late than never. Come and have something to eat."

"Oh no, I'm not ready for anything yet. I want to mooch around a bit and see if I can find Walter."

"I know exactly where you'll find him. He and Annie have been sitting in front of the band stand for ages while he's been regaling everyone with how clever he was to build the thing. Go and try to drag them away. I'm sure poor Annie must be bored out of her mind."

As he made his way towards the source of the noise in search of his friends he bumped into Sally Blower, looking very fetching in a flimsy, plunge-line dress.

"Hello, Daniel. Have you got a spare arm to support a weary lady?"

Daniel blushed slightly. He never quite knew how to handle the teasing Sally. He decided on an equally teasing response.

"Aye, Sally. You can have my arm as long as you don't lean on it too heavily. I'll need it for drinking my ale shortly."

The girl giggled with pleasure. It was the first time she had seen the humorous side of Daniel Archer. He had always been the serious one of the three brothers.

"You here on your own, Daniel?"

"Yes."

"Not got a girl yet, then?"

"I'm not looking for one, neither."

Daniel hadn't meant to sound quite so sharp, and he smiled to try to soften the harshness of his voice.

"Don't you worry none, Danny boy. You're perfectly safe with me. My husband won't be very far away and he'll be keeping an eye on me!"

She laughed at the way Daniel started at her mention of a husband.

"Didn't you know I got wed in the spring?"

"No, I hadn't heard."

"Well, I got fed up waiting for you Archer lads to ask me and I found myself a nice Borchester boy instead. I met him when I worked at that munitions factory during the war and then I saw him again at a Christmas party last year and he just up and popped the question. So I said 'yes'. Seemed the right thing to do at the time."

"Well . . . congratulations."

"Do you ever hear anything from that young brother of yours who went off to New Zealand or somewhere?"

"Frank? He's doing very well. He's working on a sheep-farm and he's been going steady for ages now. In fact, we expect to hear that he's got himself married any day now."

"I didn't mean Frank."

"Oh, Ben? Ben didn't go to New Zealand. He went to Canada."

"Yes, I remember now. How is he? Has he got married yet?"

"Not as far as we know. To tell you the truth, Sally, we don't hear all that regularly from Ben . . . just the odd note every blue moon. He keeps more in touch with his old army pal, Percy Hood. Ask Percy. He'll be able to give you more gossip about Ben."

Just then a surly looking character strode up and grabbed Sally roughly by the arm. It was her husband.

"Come on, girl. You and I are going to get ourselves something to eat before I die of starvation."

The two disappeared towards the marquee without another word to Daniel. He stared after them in bemusement.

"You've met Sally's charming husband, then?"

It was Doris Forrest. She, too, was wearing a bright summer frock, and she had a wide-brimmed straw hat over her dark curls. She looked very pretty.

"Hello, Doris. You're looking very nice."

"Thank you kindly, sir."

She dipped in a mock curtsy and smiled at him.

"This is a very nice surprise, Doris. I haven't seen you for ages. How are you?"

"I'm fine, thank you, Daniel."

Any hopes that Daniel had that Doris would be in a talkative mood looked like being dashed. Her initial friendliness had been only politeness. If there was going to be any further conversation, it would be up to him.

"Have you eaten anything yet, Doris?"

"No."

"I don't suppose you'd care to come and have something with me now?"

"Won't Jeannie mind?"

The band was getting louder and he wasn't sure that he had caught the name properly.

"Jeannie? Jeannie who?"

"Jeannie Hood . . . isn't she here today?"

"I don't know whether she's here or not. Why should I? I hardly know the girl."

"That's not what the gossip says."

"What gossip?"

"Oh, just that you've been seen around her house once or twice and that you're obviously setting your cap at her."

"Good heavens, what will they think up next? I haven't been to see Jeannie. I go and have a chat with her brother Percy every now and then. He and our Ben were old army pals, and he's the only one Ben writes to regularly. Whenever he gets a letter I go round to hear Ben's news. I don't even remember ever seeing young Jeannie when I've been there."

"So who is the lucky girl, then?"

"You might not believe it, Doris, but there isn't any girl . . . lucky or otherwise. I always seem to be too busy around the farm to have time for courting."

"Well, seeing as how you're obviously not too busy at the moment, I'll accept your kind invitation to tea in the marquee."

"Does that mean you're here on your own, too?"

"No, it doesn't . . . but I don't think my parents or Mrs Lawson-Hope will object very much if I have a cup of tea with you instead of with them."

Daniel smiled in relief. If an Ambridge girl had a sweetheart, it would be very unusual for her to be at the fete without him. Happily, he extended his arm with exaggerated courtesy in what he took to be a gentlemanly fashion, and with Doris's hand resting on it lightly they made their stately way to the marquee, both giggling with amusement.

"You two look very happy."

Daniel's mother had been standing behind the long table pouring tea from a huge pot into slightly more delicate cups. She stopped when she saw them and asked one of the other women to take her place.

"Hello, Mrs Archer. I see you've been well and truly roped in this year. Mrs Lawson-Hope's a very persuasive talker, isn't she?"

"I don't mind. It's been quite nice being on the committee. It gets me out of the house a bit more, and that stops Daniel worrying about me working too hard around the farm."

She was so pleased to see Daniel and Doris together again that she wanted to put her arms around them both, but she managed to restrain herself.

"You're looking very nice, Doris. That's a very pretty dress. Isn't it, Daniel?"

"Yes, Mother."

Doris had another fit of the giggles at Daniel's obvious embarrassment.

"I don't think Daniel's very well up on the latest fashions in women's frocks. I think he preferred Sally Blower's plunging neckline!"

"I did not."

"Then why were your eyes out like organ-stops when you were chatting to her?"

"They were not."

"Yes they were."

Phoebe was delighted. The two were reacting to each other just as they had done before the misunderstanding blew up between them. With a bit of luck Daniel would show more gumption this time and not let things dribble into the sand again.

"I think I'll leave you two to have your argument in peace. It's lovely to see you, Doris. You must bring Doris to Brookfield for tea one of these days, Daniel."

If Daniel was aware of the heavy hint from his mother, he certainly didn't show it.

Doris was more receptive.

"Thank you, Mrs Archer, that would be very nice. I would like to. It's been such an age since I was on a farm. Maybe when Daniel's not so busy, he'll show me some of the results of all his hard work?"

Mrs Archer went back to her place behind the tea table and left the couple chatting together.

"Would you really like to see round Brookfield, Doris?"

Daniel was just slightly earnest. Doris remembered why she had liked him so much.

"You are hopeless, Daniel Archer. It's you I would like to see more of, not your blooming farm."

"How do you mean, Doris?"

"Do you remember that Christmas when you were at our house for the party?"

"Of course I remember. I won't ever forget that night . . . for all sorts of reasons."

For the second time in less than an hour Daniel had been reminded of his young brother Ben and the awful row they'd had that night. He wondered if he should tell Doris about how he had fought with his brother over her. He decided against it. She wouldn't understand it all . . . why after beating his younger brother he couldn't come to her to collect "the spoils", as Ben had put it.

"That night, Daniel, you asked if I thought of you and me as sweethearts."

"Aye, I remember. You didn't give me an answer."

"I didn't give you an answer because we were interrupted by my mother, and then you never asked again. What happened? Did you lose interest? I've often thought about it and wondered what it was that made you change your mind."

"I had my mind changed for me. I thought you weren't too keen on me. As a matter of fact, I thought you were sweet on our Ben."

"Because I let him kiss me under the mistletoe? I didn't have much option, you know. He caught me completely by surprise, and once he had his arms around me I couldn't get away."

Daniel looked grim. None of the memories of that night were pleasant. He'd managed to forget at least some of them, but now the awful jealousy started nagging at him again.

"I don't really want to talk about that, if you don't mind, Doris."

"Why, Daniel Archer, I think you're jealous. Surely you can't still feel like that after all this time?"

"I don't know how I feel any more."

Doris sensed that the conversation was in danger of going in the wrong direction.

"Well, what would you have done if I'd answered your question and said that I *did* think of us as sweethearts?"

"I'd have asked you to let me talk to your folks about getting married."

"You mean you would have proposed to me?"

Doris was horrified at the lost opportunity . . . the years that had been wasted because her mother had come into the kitchen at precisely the wrong moment and because she was so young and naive.

"You couldn't have been very serious, Daniel. Was it just a whim at the time?"

Daniel decided to take his courage in both hands. The last time he had got close to proposing to Doris, he had let the chance slip away and then his stupid pride had spoiled everything. Well, two and a half years' penance was enough for any act of stupidity.

"I was very serious, Doris. I knew that I wanted to marry you but, if I'm honest, I wasn't altogether sure why. I didn't know much about love and things and I couldn't really express my feelings. That's why I went away."

"Are you telling me that I've spent the last two and a half years working as a maid at the big house when I could have been a farmer's wife?"

"I thought you liked working for Mrs Lawson-Hope?"

"I do . . . did . . . she's a very nice lady . . . but I never knew that the alternative was to be my own mistress at Brookfield."

"It's not easy being a farmer's wife, Doris. You're expected to muck in and help with everything, you know, and there's not a lot to show for all the hard work at the end of the day."

Daniel looked guiltily over his shoulder to see if anyone was listening. Nobody was, but he could see his mother watching with interest from the other side of the marquee.

"Why don't we go somewhere else to talk, Doris?"

"No, I'm not moving from this spot until we've finished this conversation. Look what happened the last time we didn't finish. You were telling me about

107

what hard work it was being a farmer's wife. Were you meaning any old farmer's wife or were you being more particular?"

"I don't understand."

"Heaven help us, Daniel Archer. Were you asking me to marry you or not?"

Daniel realised the band had stopped playing and there was a hush in the big tent. People had been listening . . . but he didn't care.

"Yes, Doris, I was. Will you marry me?"

CHAPTER ELEVEN

A scything wind swept in off the great lake, chilling the spirits of the bedraggled group of men who had gathered outside the Manitoba provincial capital building in Winnipeg. Their once-defiant placards were now being used as makeshift barriers against the cold, but were no more effective as wind-breaks than their slogans had been against unheeding politicians.

Most of the members of the group were middle aged and clearly not at home in the city. They half-heartedly waved their now-limp banners in the faces of the passers-by, and would almost certainly have dispersed hours earlier if it hadn't been for the encouragement of two younger men.

Ben Archer and Donnie Arnold had known more savage conditions. Four years before they had served together on the Western Front and had stood knee deep in the icy-cold mud of Flanders. They dismissed the Canadian November by stamping their feet, rubbing their hands and shouting a lot . . . behaviour they could never have got away with in the Battle of Ypres.

Ben Archer's Borsetshire accent stood out among the drawl of the Canadians.

"Not much longer now, lads. The beggars will be out soon. We've got to wait until then. We've got to let them know that they have a fight on their hands."

Most of the men were farm-workers from the outlying districts, and this was their first involvement with political campaigning. A few were beginning to mutter that it would be their last.

"Nobody's gonna listen to a bunch of hicks from upstate, Ben. Let's go home."

"Nobody's gonna change anything just because we say so! I say we pack up and go home, too."

"Yeh, this is stupid. I reckon we ought to leave politics to the politicians."

The constant whining made Ben angry.

"Look . . . it's already happening in Britain. The Labour Party's gaining strength all over the country. People like us can make a difference if we shout loud enough. You can't give up now!"

Donnie Arnold looked at the blazing eyes of the young Englishman and then at the cold, grey faces of his fellow Canadians. They were unhappy aliens in the hostile city. He knew that he and Ben had lost this first round of the campaign.

"We're wasting our time here, Ben. Let's go home and do something more constructive. We all want the Conservatives out, but there must be a better way than freezing our butts off."

Without waiting for any response from Ben, the rest of the men promptly dropped their placards and beat a hasty retreat to the nearest bar. Ben and Donnie gathered the boards and stacked them in a pile by the side of the main entrance to the capital building before following them. Ben didn't join the main group of drinkers, but sat disconsolately at a table in the corner toying with the pint of beer that Donnie brought over to him.

"I thought Canada was going to be so different, Donnie. When you and I talked back in Flanders, you made it sound like the land of opportunity."

Donnie remembered their conversations well. He had been in the Canadian Pioneers and had met up with Ben Archer on the long slog towards Passchendaele. Both farmers' lads, they had become good friends very quickly and often spent the long cold nights regaling each other with the wonders of their respective homes . . . the hundred acres of Brookfield and the two thousand prairie acres of the Winnipegosis Ranch. Donnie smiled as he remembered one particular night when they had argued about which was the better soil, the dark brown of Manitoba or the rich red of Borsetshire. Someone, obviously bored by the agricultural content of the dialogue, had loudly threatened to drown them both in the black, stinking mud of Flanders.

"From what I remember, Ben, you thought your little Ambridge place was pretty special, too. So why aren't you back there raising your wheat and your kids?"

"That's a long story, Donnie. Maybe I'll tell you about it one day."

Since he had come to Canada at the beginning of 1919, meeting up with Donnie again was the only good thing that had happened to Ben. He had arrived expecting to be able to walk straight into a farming job – he knew that the farms here were huge by English standards, each employing dozens of men. What he hadn't realised was that the slump that was just beginning to affect Britain when he left home was also hitting Canada, and that the farmers were suffering exactly the same squeeze between falling grain prices and the high cost of living. Like thousands of other hopeful immigrants, Ben had discovered the hard way that jobs were few and far between.

With only a few pounds in his pocket, he had been forced to take work wherever he could find it. For a couple of months he had helped to lay the track for a new railroad that was being built between Winnipeg and Fort William, five hundred miles away in Ontario. It was back-breaking, exhausting work but he found some compensation in the rough, tough, roistering company of the other gangers. He would probably have stayed on for the whole project if the company hadn't gone bust.

After that, he managed to find a handyman's job in a lumber camp on the edge of Lake Winnipeg. To Ben the lake looked as big as an ocean, and the scenery around the camp was breathtaking. For some reason the spectacular views made him homesick for the first time, and he realised that he was more than four thousand miles from Ambridge. On top of that, the work he was expected to do was humiliating. He had to

111

peel potatoes, wash dishes, mop floors and even clean out stinking lavatories . . . and always at the times when the lumberjacks were enjoying their limited leisure with hard drinking and carousing. As a drudge, he would never have been welcome in their company.

When he couldn't stand it any longer, Ben left the camp and made tracks back to Winnipeg where all he could get was a labourer's job in a big factory. Again he found the work soul-destroying, and he was quite pleased when the metal-workers went on strike and the factory closed down. He wasn't so happy when he discovered that he was caught in the middle of one of the city's most savage industrial wars which soon spread to other factories and then even to the public services, including the police.

The effect of the strike was to make jobs even more difficult to find. To try to take the edge off his despair and boredom, Ben started attending some of the strikers' meetings, and the rousing political speeches he heard struck home with him. It was time, said the strikers' leaders, for an end to the old politics of the Conservative and Liberal Parties. They hadn't been responsive enough to the changes in Canadian society; new directions must be found if the gap between the haves and the have-nots was to be bridged.

It was while he was at a crowded meeting listening to one of these speeches that Ben met a young farm-worker who told him he came from Winnipegosis. The odd-sounding name rang a bell, and he remembered that it was where Donnie Arnold had said he lived. To Ben's surprise, the man knew the Arnold ranch and offered to take him back there in the hope of getting a job.

Ben was never sure which of the two of them was the more surprised at their reunion, but Donnie gave him a terrific reception and insisted that he stayed at the ranch-house for a couple of weeks' rest before he would even talk about work. Ben's name had obviously cropped up in Donnie's accounts of his own war

112

exploits, and his parents were ready to treat him like a conquering hero. For two weeks he lived like a king, fussed over by Mrs Arnold and encouraged by Mr Arnold and Donnie to reminisce about army days and recount his experiences since coming to Canada.

During these conversations, it became quite clear that young Donnie shared Ben's political convictions. Like his father, he was a member of the huge Grain Growers' Association, and from them Ben learned that there was clearly discontent, even among the biggest farmers, over the way the government was treating agriculture.

Once Ben was settled into the communal bunkhouse and had established himself as a reliable, hard-working ranch-hand, Donnie persuaded him to make a trip with him back to Winnipeg so that Ben could introduce him to some of the strikers there. The outcome was that both of them joined the new National Progressive Party.

Donnie's social standing and his energy, combined with Ben's idealism and passion, made them a formidable team. The Party's provincial leaders persuaded the two of them to set about forming an upstate local branch, and they had soon gathered a substantial membership. However, operating out in the countryside, they felt somewhat isolated, and this afternoon's demonstration had been an attempt to bring their members closer to the main Party.

It was Donnie who was supposed to have made the arrangements with the city branch organisers for their members to join the demonstration, but he had never got round to it. No one but their own members had turned up. At first Ben had been angry, but now he was more anxious that his companions would be discouraged by the afternoon's events, and that the plan to involve them more clearly had back-fired.

"We'll never be able to make progress if the men go home and tell everyone what a waste of time this has all been."

"Don't be so pessimistic, Ben. You don't know these guys like I do. Don't forget – none of them has ever done anything like this before, and they still can't see the point of standing around cold sidewalks waiting for a bunch of gasbags to finish their boring discussions so that we can wave a few placards under their noses."

Ben found it hard to understand that not all working men might have the same commitment as he had to social change, and he shook his head in exasperation as he watched the group down pint after pint. They certainly didn't look like the political agitators they would no doubt be labelled by the newspapers.

"Now I know how Keir Hardie must have felt in the early days of the Labour Party back in Britain."

"Come on, Ben. Give it a rest. Let's get into the truck and get the men back to Winnipegosis. Then you can come up to the house for a bite of supper and we can have a chat with Dad and see if he has any ideas about where we should go from here."

On the long, cold, bumpy ride back, Ben said very little. He had expected to be feeling elated, and the anticlimax of the day hit him very hard. He didn't cheer up until he went up to the ranch-house and discovered that some friends of the Arnolds had come to stay for a few days, bringing their very attractive daughter with them. The Delamaines were from Quebec and spoke with an accent that reminded Ben of the Belgians he had met during the war.

Simone was probably a couple of years younger than Ben. During supper he was unexpectedly relieved to see that Donnie regarded her as a sister. She had never met an Englishman before and kept giggling at Ben's accent and what she described as the "funny words" he used.

When she heard that he and Donnie were involved with politics, she became much more serious and asked if either of them read the new magazine *Canada Forum*. Donnie laughed and said he didn't have time to read magazines, but Ben felt obliged to excuse his ignorance of the magazine on the grounds of his being an immigrant. He didn't want Simone to know that he'd hardly read more than half a dozen books in his whole life and that his newspaper reading had been confined to the *Ypres Times* when he was in Flanders and the *Daily Mirror* when he was at home in England.

"I'm afraid I haven't caught up with that one yet."

"Then you must remedy that, monsieur. It is a very interesting publication that is regularly quite critical of the established politicians, especially Mr Meighen, the prime minister, but also the leader of the Liberals, Mr King."

Ben was less concerned with the personalities of the Party leaders than with the kind of feudalistic system they represented. In fact, until now he hadn't even known their names. He was beginning to realise that there were too many things he didn't know.

"Have you read Stephen Leacock?"

If Simone Delamaine thought she was making polite conversation, she was very much mistaken. Poor Ben blushed in embarrassment. He had no idea what or who was Stephen Leacock.

"No . . . I don't think so."

"Ah, Monsieur Archer, I can see your education of matters Canadian is sadly lacking. If you are to become a new politician, shouldn't you be learning more about us?"

"Yes . . . I suppose you're right."

By now, Ben was totally captivated by the young French Canadian and found her accent fascinating. He would have agreed with her about almost anything just as long as she kept speaking to him.

"Let me help you in the matter of Stephen Leacock. He is one of our best writers and he has published a book called *Sunshine Sketches of a Little Town*. I mention it only because I think you will enjoy it very much. He writes with some wit about the pettiness of life in the town. As a countryman, would you not appreciate such observations?"

"It sounds very interesting."

"You may find it difficult to buy because it was published quite a few years ago, but if you are interested I could lend you my copy when I come next time to Winnipegosis."

Later that night, Ben lay in the bunkhouse and thought about Simone Delamaine. He had never met anyone quite like her. None of the girls he had known in the past had been even remotely interested in politics. She was very attractive and obviously very clever. Too clever for the likes of him? She hadn't seemed to mind that he hadn't read any of the books or magazines she had mentioned. Maybe he could get hold of some of them before she came back?

The other thing about the girl that had impressed him very much was her total lack of concern that he was only a ranch-hand. He was always conscious of being spoken down to – wasn't that why he was getting involved in politics? – but she hadn't done that. She was practising the very philosophy that he preached. Perhaps she was just being polite? Was her promise to bring him the Stephen Leacock book just politeness, or did she really mean it?

Ben found himself hoping very hard that she did. For the first time in years he felt there could be an end to his restlessness. He very much wanted to see Simone Delamaine again . . . and not just to talk to about books and politics.

For no reason that he could explain, Ben suddenly remembered the letter that he'd had the week before from his brother, Daniel. He'd had quite a few letters from home since he'd been in Canada, but had replied to only a couple. He was a hopeless letter-writer because he never knew what to say. He could never explain why he had been so anxious to get away from Ambridge, and he felt that it was better to leave everyone there in peace and not have them worrying about him.

Not replying to letters had become a habit, but this most recent one was different. Daniel had said that he and Doris Forrest were finally getting married, and that if he could possibly get home they would like him to be best man. Well, there was no hope of his being able to get back to England – would he ever do that again, he wondered – but he could do the next best thing. Tomorrow he would find some paper and write a letter.

The Spenser Mountains were more than fifty miles away but, shading his eyes against the bright November sunshine, Frank Archer could see their soaring peaks etched very clearly against the cloudless blue sky. Birds sang, and all around him the sheep were bleating noisily. Whenever he felt that he might have made a mistake in coming to New Zealand, this was the sort of day that changed his mind.

Frank was very happy at his work, helping to look after the huge herd owned by sheep-farmer Samuel Wilson, but every now and then he still felt great twinges of homesickness . . . just like yesterday, when he'd had that letter asking if there were any chance of his going home to Ambridge for Daniel's wedding.

He always felt bad when he saw the Borchester postmark on letters, perhaps because he had never properly recovered from the first letter he ever received from his mother. It had been waiting for him after the weeks-long voyage from England to New Zealand, and it told him that his father had died.

He went cold as he remembered the awfulness of that day. He had arrived at the Wilson farm exhausted with all the travelling and bewildered by the strangeness of being so far from home. Mrs Wilson had given him the letter more or less as he walked through the door because she thought it would cheer him up a bit. He had happily ripped open the envelope, expecting to read all the latest gossip from Ambridge. He was almost eighteen, but there was nothing he could do to stop himself bursting into tears.

The Wilsons were very sympathetic and packed him off to bed, where he lay for hours sobbing his heart out and feeling somehow responsible for his father's death. If he hadn't insisted on leaving Ambridge his father wouldn't have had to work so hard. If he hadn't had to work so hard, he wouldn't have died of a heart attack.

He also felt guilty that he wasn't there to help his mother, that he had run out on her. He wanted to go straight back, but Samuel Wilson had persuaded him that there was nothing he could do if he did, and that in any case Daniel would probably be back from France already.

From somewhere he gained the courage to heed the advice and to stay on in Culverdon. Now, the little township about a hundred miles north of Christchurch had become his home. After more than three years he was beginning to feel and sound like a New Zealander. The sun had darkened his skin and the last traces of his gentle Borchester accent came out only when he was excited.

Frank made a mental note that he must write to Daniel to apologise for not being able to attend his wedding. He smiled at the thought of being the best man. It could have been good fun, except for the speeches. He wouldn't have liked that part very much, and would probably have made a mess of it. He wondered if Ben would get back from Canada. Probably not. It wouldn't be any easier for him than it would be for Frank to make the long journey.

"Frank!"

He heard his name being called from the farmhouse. It was Mrs Wilson letting him know that Sunday lunch was ready. The Wilsons were themselves immigrants from England, and even after twenty years in New Zealand they still kept up the old traditions. Sunday lunch was one of them.

Frank had been very lucky in landing a job with Samuel Wilson. The farmer had only the one child – a little girl called Laura, who Frank guessed was probably about ten years old now – and he had more or less adopted Frank as a son, insisting that he live in the house as one of the family.

Apart from the obvious advantages of making him feel that he had a real home, there were other benefits – and those included plenty of opportunities for Samuel to pass on his almost encyclopaedic knowledge of sheep. Usually this happened when they were working together in the pens, but sheep were also a regular topic of conversation on Sunday afternoons.

Another regular subject at the table was politics. Samuel was a supporter of the Reform Party and was keen that young Frank and anyone else who would listen should understand why.

"It's the farmers' Party!"

Frank was uninterested in politics but he always managed to hide the fact because he didn't want to offend Mr Wilson.

"Why is that? Because the prime minister was a farmer?"

"No, no, Frank. Bill Massey wasn't just a farmer, although he did have one of the biggest dairy herds on North Island. He had the right idea about giving New Zealand back to the people who deserve a bit of it! It was Bill Massey and his men who made it possible for me to own Culverdon Farm instead of just being a tenant working for the state."

Frank had heard it all before, but it never convinced him that politics or politicians had any part in his life, although he had difficulty persuading some people of that when they heard that he had come to New Zealand instead of joining up. They immediately wanted to stick the label 'pacifist' around his neck and rail at him for being a left-winger.

That's not how he saw himself. He just didn't want to be party to killing other people, whoever they were or whatever they had done. If that meant he had to accept being called a pacifist, that was just too bad. But he would not agree that he was a left-winger. He didn't quite understand what it meant, but assumed it was something like a communist and he certainly wasn't one of them. He'd heard all about the communists and their subversive activities during the great rows that used to take place between his father, a diehard Liberal, and Ben, who was convinced that the Labour Party had the only answers to Britain's problems.

He often wondered what Ben and Daniel thought about his decision not to join up. He regretted not having been able to talk to them about it before he made his decision, but he hadn't started thinking about it until long after they had both gone off to France. His parents had both been very good about it, but he could never be sure whether or not they understood his reasons.

When he had first arrived in New Zealand he used to try to explain his feelings to people who argued with him, but that seemed to make them even angrier. Their line was that nearly seventeen thousand New Zealand boys had died in the war, and that he should be ashamed of himself for not joining up like them. Instead of quoting the death statistics back at them as part of his case exposing the futility of war, Frank learned to keep his mouth shut and let others say what they wanted.

Listening to Mr Wilson going on about the Reform Party, he decided to try to change the subject.

"You were telling me that you were going to get in some new sheep. What did you say they were, Southdales?"

"Yes, that's right, and they're a fascinating breed. They come from our own New Zealand Corriedales crossed with Old English Southdowns."

By the end of lunch Frank had learned that the Corriedales had originally been bred in New Zealand from Lincoln rams and Merino ewes, that the Lincolns had originated in Belgium, and that the Merinos, which he thought were Australian, had come from North Africa. He knew already that the Southdowns came from Sussex and were the oldest breed of sheep in

England, and he also knew that the other local favourites, the long-wool Romneys, were first raised back in Kent. If he had stayed at home in Ambridge, he doubted if he would have learned as much in a lifetime as he had in an hour or so at Samuel Wilson's dining table.

Later, sitting outside the back door of the farmhouse where little Laura was playing with her dog, Frank looked up again at the Spenser Mountains. All that seemed to lie between them and the farm were sheep. It was an idyllic scene. New Zealand would do for him, he thought.

CHAPTER TWELVE

The sweet smell of winter flowers filled the church and the organ swelled to the strains of the traditional Wedding March. Doris Forrest, on the arm of her proud father, floated serenely down the aisle in a gentle flurry of white organdie and lace. Behind her, unsure of her bridesmaid's duties and for want of something better to do, Lisa Scroby fussed over the hem of the long, trailing skirt of the bridal gown.

Waiting at the altar, Daniel Archer was calm and unflustered, but looked slightly ill at ease in his stiff, new, dark grey suit. Beside him, Walter Gabriel, enormously pleased with himself, could easily have been mistaken for the groom rather than the best man. He, too, had invested in a new suit, but he obviously didn't trust the pockets and held the gold wedding ring in his tightly clenched fist.

In the front pew on the bride's side of the church Lisa Forrest sat wet-eyed as she remembered her own wedding day. She looked proudly at her husband in *his* best suit, ready to give Doris away, and she felt so happy for her daughter on this day of all days. But she still missed her elder son Teddy terribly. It was only two years since his funeral had been held in St Stephen's. Young Tommy looked bored in his place at her side. Just eleven, he would rather have been out in the bell tower, for he had just embarked on a life-long enthusiasm for the art of bell-ringing.

Phoebe Archer, on the bridegroom's side, hid her emotions, as usual. She was delighted to see Daniel finally standing at the altar . . . waiting to be joined by the girl she had always hoped he would marry. But her happiness was mixed with sadness that her husband wasn't alive to witness their eldest son's wedding with her, and she was desperately disappointed that neither Ben nor Frank had been able to get back for the occasion.

Despite the bitter cold in this week before Christmas, the church was packed with villagers, some of them friends and relatives of the two families, others just come out of curiosity to see who had or had not been invited, and who was wearing what.

At the altar rail the vicar waited patiently for the slow procession down the aisle. His finger was wedged between the appropriate pages in his order of service because he had misplaced the leather bookmark that usually did the job. He winced slightly as the organist missed another note but was relieved that no one else appeared to notice. Enthusiastic worshippers his parishioners might be; musical they were not. Sometimes he came to church on Sundays with his heart heavy in the knowledge that a few more beautiful hymns would be murdered that morning.

Occasional whispers could be heard at the back of the church, and coughs acted as punctuation marks in the hushed atmosphere. Somewhere a child started to chatter, but was quickly stifled by an embarrassed parent. Instead of the hefty clip around the ear that would usually have been meted out, being in church more subtle means were called for, and the rest of the congregation heard the unmistakable sound of a sweet being noisily unwrapped and even more noisily sucked.

At last the bride reached the altar. The vicar began the service, intoning the solemn lines of the marriage service, and Doris and Daniel responded parrot-fashion in the prescribed places, as they had been instructed. The ring was safely prised from Walter Gabriel's sweating palm and placed by Daniel on Doris's finger, and the vicar delivered the traditional homily, bidding the happy couple to follow the path of God, and wishing them well on their journey through life. Then, the formalities over, Mr and Mrs Daniel Archer took their first steps together on that journey, walking together up the aisle and out into the church porch.

Snatches of comment surrounded them from all sides as Daniel hugged his new wife and received the congratulations of his family and neighbours.

"What a lovely bride."

"Doesn't she look beautiful."

"That's a lovely dress."

"The squire's mother made it."

"Daniel Archer looks very handsome in his suit."

"He looks very pleased with himself."

"So he should. He's got himself a grand wife."

He felt very happy, and there was so much he wanted to say to them all. He wanted to tell everybody that he knew he was a lucky man. He wanted to tell them, too, that he knew how pretty Doris was and what a gentle person she was. He wanted to say that he knew she was a hard-working lass and he'd tasted enough of her cooking to be more than satisfied in that department. He wanted to say that he knew he had found the perfect farmer's wife.

He didn't say any of these things. He was too overwhelmed by the occasion. Instead he settled for smiling hugely as his hand was pumped furiously by dozens of well-wishers, most of whom added a great slap on the back for good measure.

Doris couldn't quite believe that she was now a married woman. She had reached the age of twenty-one without a single proposal and had begun to feel that she was doomed to be a spinster. No wonder she had forced Daniel's hand when she bumped into him at the village fete just a week after that all-important birthday!

Whenever she thought about it afterwards, she blushed at her own forwardness on that occasion. But today her blushes were simply those of a happy bride. She knew that her secret was safe with her new husband.

The road to the altar hadn't been altogether smooth for Daniel and Doris. Things had appeared bad enough during the long, empty years when they had been kept apart by misunderstandings, but as soon as they had declared their intentions to wed, life had become one endless debate. When? Where? Who was to be bridesmaid . . . best man? What music should they choose? Where would the reception be? Who should be invited? Hundreds of questions asked, hundreds of decisions to be taken.

At one stage Daniel was so confused by all the discussions that he had wanted to call the whole thing off. But Walter Gabriel, knowing by then that he was to be the best man and determined not to miss his moment of glory, insisted that nothing should prevent the wedding from going ahead. He had talked so hard and so loud that, even if Daniel hadn't wanted to marry Doris, he would probably have conceded the argument rather than put up with Walter's constant tirades. Of course, there never *was* any doubt in his mind; he did want to marry Doris – but he could have done without all the fuss.

Daniel hadn't easily got agreement for his choice of Walter as best man. Phoebe had still hoped that either Ben or Frank would be able to get home for the wedding; if one of them did, then he must have the honour. Doris wasn't too keen on Walter either, because, she said, he was always so noisy and restless. He was bound to lose the ring or do something silly. She wanted Daniel to ask Silas Winter, one of his old classmates at the village school, now head stable lad on the estate. She reasoned that he would be able to provide them with a lucky horseshoe, but Daniel said that he could get a hundred horseshoes and he didn't see why he should ask Silas. Walter eventually won the day.

Picking a bridesmaid was only slightly easier. It was amazing how many cousins were suddenly conjured out of nowhere when there was a wedding in the air. Mrs Forrest produced a long list of possible candidates, and Doris was upset because it didn't include any of her personal friends. Out of devilment she had suggested

Sally Blower-that-was, insisting that she would look lovely in a low-cut bridesmaid's dress. Daniel, unaware that he was being teased, was outraged. He was less concerned when Mrs Forrest suggested either Rosemary or Polly Winyard. They were twins, and regarded by most people as local beauties. He didn't know them very well, but had always thought they were nice enough girls. Either of them would do. No, they wouldn't, said Doris. She wanted Lisa Scroby and, of course, Lisa Scroby was who she had.

The choice of a date had caused a few headaches, too. Daniel had so many reasons for not being able to get away from the farm that Doris began to think he was trying to find an excuse for backing out. When he finally had agreed on a day, both his mother and Lisa Forrest objected that it would be too close to Christmas. Doris, however, would not be gainsaid, and the vicar had innocently fallen in with her by pointing out that the seventeenth of December was the only free Saturday he had for months.

There hadn't been any disagreement over the place. Every Ambridge bride was married in the village church – anywhere else would have been unthinkable. The music and hymns were also decided without too much argument. Doris had a very strong musical bent; everyone seemed happy to leave the choice to her.

It was the wedding reception that had caused the most anxiety. It had seemed a simple enough matter to start with . . . until Mrs Lawson-Hope said she would like to give Doris a reception at the Manor House, as a wedding gift. No one disputed that it was a very kind gesture, but William Forrest would have none of it. The reception was the bride's father's responsibility and he was the bride's father. Lady of the manor or not, he would not allow Mrs Lawson-Hope to step in and show him up in front of the whole village. Folk would think he couldn't afford to give his only daughter a proper send-off. Daniel understood that argument quite clearly, but Doris didn't. She said if Mrs Lawson-Hope was good enough to offer all the facilities of the big house, it would be very rude not to accept – and, in any case, no one quite knew how to broach the subject of William's objections with her.

In the end it was the squire who solved the problem. He overheard one of their servants talking about it, and immediately spoke to his mother. Angry with herself for not having been more considerate of William Forrest's feelings, she sent for Doris to explain that she hadn't given the matter proper thought. She had simply thought that arranging the reception in the Manor House would have saved Doris's parents a great deal of time and trouble, but she apologised profusely for causing so much upset and asked if she might be allowed to offer a more appropriate wedding present; it turned out to be a beautiful bone-china tea service.

Outside the church, as the photographer carefully posed the different groups for the formal photographs, all the fuss and bother was forgotten. The grey December clouds had thinned out, and a watery sun was doing its best to raise the temperature above freezing point.

"Just one more shot, please."

The photographer dived under the black cloth of his huge camera.

"Stand very still. Don't move, now. Smile. That's lovely. No, no. You moved, Mrs Archer . . . Mrs Archer senior, that is. I'm sorry, but can we do it just once again. Now please, very still this time. Hold it . . . hold it . . . please. Lovely . . . I've got it!"

With a final flash the photographic session was over and the guests made their way across the green to the village hall where William Forrest had arranged a splendid reception for his daughter. The members of the Women's Institute had already decorated the hall ready for the Christmas festivities, and it looked very pretty with lots of holly and fir cones.

A long table groaned with food of every description. William Forrest had ceaselessly nagged Lisa to make sure there would be plenty for all the guests, and now there seemed to be enough to feed the whole of Borsetshire. The centrepiece of the spread was a magnificent two-tiered cake that Percy Hood had baked and decorated himself as a gift to the couple. He maintained that he had learned to tackle cake decorating while he had been in the army, but from all the stories he had to tell of his days in the trenches no one was able to work out when he could have had the time!

"Ladies and gentlemen, it is my very great honour today to act as best master and man of ceremonies . . . er, best man and master of ceremonies at this celebration of the wedding of my very good friends, Daniel Archer and Doris Forrest . . . er, Forrest that was . . . now, of course, Doris Archer."

Poor Walter Gabriel had spent hours practising his speech, but he'd lost all his notes; the roars of laughter told him that he'd made a mess of things almost from the word go.

"Oh heck, let's forget all the formalities. You all know as how I'm not exactly practised in public speaking, but if I'm to do right by me old pal Daniel and me old beauty, Doris . . . I'm sorry, Doris love, I don't mean old . . . oh heck. What I means is, can I introduce the bride's father, who will say a few words? Mr Forrest!"

To great cheers and lots of good-natured mockery, Walter gratefully sat down, and pulled out a bright red handkerchief to mop the sweat from his brow . . . bringing the missing notes flying out with it! It was too late – now it was William Forrest's turn to suffer from stage-fright. He had also made some notes, but his hand was shaking so much that he couldn't read them.

"Friends . . . I might be a lot older than young Walter Gabriel, but . . . er . . . when it comes to this sort of thing . . . I mean, speaking in public . . . I have no more experience than he has."

There was a long pause as he stared at his notes and tried to control his shaking hand. Doris, who had laughed quite happily as Walter had come to grief, suddenly felt embarrassed at her father's discomfort.

"Can't you get up and speak now, Daniel? My dad's not going to manage to say anything sensible."

Daniel, however, was not to be moved before it was the proper moment for him.

"I can't interrupt your dad, love."

"You wouldn't be interrupting. He isn't saying anything. Oh, Daniel, please do something before I die of shame."

"Don't be daft. No one expects a great speech at a wedding. The folk are just happy to be here."

William Forrest had come to the same decision.

"Friends . . . you won't expect much talk from me. You know I'm a man of few words . . . but I want to tell you that Daniel Archer has got himself the best wife in the whole of Ambridge. I know you'll think I'm saying that because she's my daughter. Well, that's not true. I mean, she *is* my daughter . . . that *is* true . . . the bit that's not true is that I'm just saying nice things about her because she is . . . my daughter."

The ale that was taking its toll of William Forrest had already deadened the wits of most of the other men sitting around the tables. None of them seemed to notice his confusion. Of the women, only Doris and her mother looked anxious.

"Please, Daniel, do something. Please."

"In a minute, Doris. In a minute. I've got to wait for Walter to call on me before I can speak."

Forgetting his own stammering performance, Walter chose that moment to rescue the bride's father and stood up to resume his best man's duties, much to Doris's relief. She even felt grateful that she'd been outvoted in the argument about best man.

"Ladies and gentlemen . . . a round of applause for Mr Forrest."

Unsure of whether or not he had finished his speech, William Forrest looked across at Walter, decided that he probably had, and collapsed into his chair amid a spluttering of half-hearted claps and a few cheers.

"Now, ladies and gentlemen . . . it's my duty to call upon the bridegroom to say a few words . . . me old pal, Farmer Dan Archer."

Knowing how tongue-tied he could get, Daniel had prepared what he wanted to say very carefully. As he rose to his feet, he produced a sheaf of neatly written notes from his pocket. Like Walter, he had been practising half the morning, and although he felt very nervous he thought he'd be able to cope . . . just. He fidgeted with his tie and glanced down at his new wife for encouragement.

"Squire, Mrs Lawson-Hope, ladies and gentlemen. My wife and I . . ."

Loud cheers broke out, and Doris blushed. Daniel grinned in relief. Emboldened by having broken the ice, Daniel restarted with more confidence.

"My wife and I feel very honoured that you have all seen fit to come to join us on this very special occasion. This is a very important day for me, and I hope it is for Doris, too."

Doris blushed again but nodded her assent.

"You all know that one of the most important decisions a farmer has to make is over the girl he chooses to be his wife . . . because a farmer's wife isn't just a wife. She's a partner . . . someone to share the work of the farm and all the responsibilities that go with rearing animals and seeding crops.

"I pondered long and hard before I picked my partner. Some of you might have thought I spent so much time thinking that I would never get round to it. Well, now I have and I know you'll all agree with me that I've made a wise choice.

"You can all see for yourselves how pretty she is, and you can all see that she's a fine figure of a woman who won't buckle under the weight of the odd bag of potatoes or a pitchfork full of wet hay. Mrs Lawson-Hope will,

I'm sure, testify that she is also loyal and hard-working. She is, in fact, the perfect farmer's wife, and I'm very, very proud that she consented to be this particular farmer's wife."

Mistaking Daniel's pause for breath as the end of his speech, Walter Gabriel leapt to his feet and led the applause that echoed around the hall. Daniel decided to quit while he was winning and quietly pocketed the rest of his notes. Doris looked very proud.

"That was a lovely speech, Daniel. Do you really think I'll make a good farmer's wife?"

"Of course I do, Doris. I meant every word of what I said . . . and more. You and me are going to make a smashing team at Brookfield. Folk say as how it's a good farm already. Well, wait until we really get going. We'll make it the best in the whole area. I've got big plans for us."

Before Daniel could say anything else, Walter was back on his feet, determined to give full value as master of ceremonies. He started reading out messages and short letters from some of the people who hadn't been able to attend the wedding.

There were two letters that he didn't read out . . . because he hadn't been told about them. They were from Frank and Ben, and had arrived within a few days of each other about a week or so earlier. Daniel had shown them only to his mother and to Doris. They were now safely in a drawer at home, but Daniel had been so pleased to receive them that he'd read them over and over again, and knew every word by heart.

The first one had come from New Zealand:

Dear Daniel,
Everyone tells me married life is just great. I'm sure you'll enjoy getting cups of tea every five minutes of the day and there are other benefits which I can't write about but which I'm sure will mean that you have an extra happy Christmas.

It was really great news to hear that you were marrying at long last. I honestly can't remember

Doris Forrest very well because she was already working at the big house when I was old enough to notice girls! I'm sure she must be very nice if you picked her as a wife.

I'm sorry that I won't be able to take up the invitation to the wedding but it would just take too much money for fares and the time that I would have to take off work. I would have liked to come home very much because I still miss you all, and it would have been quite an excuse to see you again, especially you and Mother. Give her my love and tell her I will write to her very soon.

It was signed simply "Frank", and had a postscript:

Is Ben going to get home?

Daniel was very sad that the answer to that question was "no", but Ben's letter had softened the blow considerably. It had been postmarked in Winnipeg, Canada.

Dear Danny,
This letter is long overdue, but that was partly because I didn't know what to say to you and partly because, as you know, I have always had great difficulty in sitting down and concentrating long enough to put two thoughts together. I have already started this letter about a dozen times, which will give you some idea of how hard it is for me.

What I want to say, Danny Boy, is that I really am delighted that you and Doris are getting together at long last. I never could understand why you didn't make any move as soon as I left Brookfield. I mean, don't forget that's one of the reasons why I left! Still, you always were a slow beggar when it came to things like courting the girls.

I have felt guilty that you not marrying Doris before now had something to do with me. If that's so, I am very sorry. I was very mixed up, and a lot of the things I said were out of bitterness about that

132

bloody war. Fortunately, I've got it all out of my system now, and the politicians over here don't seem to be quite as two-faced as the British ones were at the end of the war.

I still think I was right about there not being enough for both of us at Brookfield and I have no regrets at leaving. The way I left wasn't very nice and I often feel ashamed, which is probably another reason for not writing this letter before.

This is already the longest letter I have ever written in my entire life and I still haven't mentioned Doris properly, or Mother.

Doris is a lovely girl and you are a lucky man to be marrying her. I know she will make you a grand wife and I wish you both good luck in your future together. I wish I could be back in Ambridge for the wedding, but it just isn't possible for a whole lot of reasons that I won't bore you with.

Try to explain to Mother for me that going away and not writing doesn't mean that I don't care about her. I really do, but I just never know how to put things into a letter properly, as you can tell from this particular disjointed effort. Maybe some civilian will come up with the equivalent of the old army field-postcard and that will make it easier for people like me to keep in touch with their families.

Well, again good luck, Danny Boy. Give my love to Doris.

Your loving brother,

Ben

PS I was right . . . to the victor, the spoils!

CHAPTER THIRTEEN

The little snug bar of The Bull was unusually quiet for the night before the harvest festival. Only two tables were occupied. Percy Hood and George Grundy sat at one playing dominoes, while Bill Sawyer, Silas Winter and Daniel Archer were chatting around the other one. Behind the bar, Jake Burton looked morose as he aimlessly polished glasses and waited for other customers.

Normally the pub would have been packed with farmers from all over the district, come to boast of their bumper harvest and to oil their tonsils in readiness for the traditional harvest hymns that would be sung the next evening in St Stephen's.

This year was different. This year, Britain's farmers were beginning to realise that the golden years were over. The new economic depression had begun to bite, and the problems had been savagely brought home to the folk in Ambridge that day by the unexplained death of Jesse Plant of Wimberton Farm, out on the Penny Hassett road.

He had been found dead in one of his barns. Most people said he had killed himself because of his terrible financial worries, but no one would know the truth until the coroner had held the inquest the following week.

Jesse had enjoyed life as the tenant at Wimberton for more than twenty years, and during that time had built up a very successful business that employed eight full-time labourers. When the chance came for him to buy the farm, he had jumped at it.

Like hundreds of other farmers around the country, he had simply taken advantage of a situation that was forcing many landowners to sell off thousands of acres. Big estates were having to be broken up because of the new and crippling death duties that had been introduced towards the end of the war. Someone had been reported in the paper as saying that between six and eight million acres had changed hands in less than four years.

To buy the farm, Jesse had had to take out a fairly hefty mortgage . . . and that was the beginning of his problems. The repayments were a constant worry, but he had managed reasonably well for the first couple of years because the government's price guarantees had assured a good income from the crops. The trouble really began when the politicians changed their minds about subsidies and, as George Grundy was always fond of saying, the farmers were thrown to the wolves. Not too many people around Ambridge disagreed with him on this occasion.

"Who do you think is going to be next?"

The starkness of George Grundy's question startled everyone in the bar. Jake Burton polished his glasses even more furiously, and Percy Hood concentrated hard on the line of dominoes in front of him. It was Daniel Archer who replied.

"That's not healthy talk, George. Things aren't all that bad. Farmers have known worse times."

George Grundy grimaced and downed the remains of his pint.

"You try telling that to Jesse Plant's widow and kids. They won't get the insurance money, the farm will have to be sold from under them, and they won't even have a place to live."

Percy Hood, who knew more than most about local people's financial problems at first hand because so many of them had run up big bills at his bakery, tapped a domino impatiently.

"Come on, George, give it a rest. We've all come out for a bit of peace and quiet. No one wants to go on about how hard things are. Times are hard for all of us. Besides, we don't know yet if it's true that poor Jesse killed himself."

George, however, was not in a mood to be silenced by the likes of the local baker.

"It's true enough, I'd say. He'd been in trouble for over a year now. You know yourself he started cutting his

135

men's wages in January . . . cut them back from their miserable forty bob a week to less than thirty, he did."

Bill Sawyer's younger brother was one of the eight hands who worked at Wimberton Farm as a labourer. He knew that George Grundy was right.

"Some of the lads got cut back even further than that, and only last week Jesse was talking about laying off some of them altogether."

"Well, they'll certainly be laid off right enough now, won't they?"

Daniel Archer could see an argument looming and decided he didn't want to be part of it. He drained his glass and got up to leave.

"What's the matter, Daniel? Haven't got the stomach for a discussion that might be a bit hard on your friend the squire and his well-off cronies?"

George Grundy was an awkward enough character at the best of times. With a couple of pints under his belt he could be positively nasty. His jibe stung Daniel, who promptly sat down again.

"George Lawson-Hope is a nice bloke, and although he isn't what you could call a friend I'd be very happy if he were. In any case, I don't see how you or anybody else can hold the squire responsible for what happened to poor Jesse. Jesse was a proud man, and he would have worried himself sick about doing his men down, and even more about having to put them out of work. If what happened to him wasn't some awful accident, it would have been his pride that made him decide to take such a course. You can't blame one man for another man's pride!"

Silas Winter intervened.

"Don't get riled, Daniel. You know what George is like when he's had a few."

George Grundy became even more truculent.

"You just be careful with that mouth of yours, Silas Winter. It could get you into a lot of trouble. Don't you go insinuating that I'm a drunk or you and I might have to step outside."

Jake Burton, slightly nervous at the prospect of a row, decided to pour ale on troubled waters.

"All right everyone. Just calm down and you can all have a half-pint on the house."

The limit of the landlord's generosity to half-pints tickled everybody in the bar. They all laughed, breaking the tension. George Grundy offered an olive branch.

"I'm sorry, Silas. I didn't mean to get personal. You too, Daniel. I really didn't mean to upset you."

"That's all right, George. I know how strongly you feel."

"That's the problem. I do feel very strongly about things, and no one ever seems to want to talk about what's happening. Everyone seems to think that if they keep their heads down, it can't happen to them. Well, it can . . . and Jesse Plant has just proved that, hasn't he? The problem isn't just the usual hot air you read in the newspapers. It's happening right here in Ambridge."

Daniel couldn't remember ever having heard George Grundy in this kind of mood. He'd seen him angry often enough, but this time the anger was mixed with a genuine anxiety; it seemed he really did want to talk rather than to argue.

"If you want to have a sensible conversation, then I'm sure we're all more than happy to join in."

There was a chorus of agreement from the others. Jake Burton looked relieved and celebrated by serving them all pints instead of the promised halves.

"The thing is, I think that there are a number of farmers around here who're in just as much trouble as poor Jesse but are afeared of letting on about it. I reckon there's more trouble on the way. I run my place single-handed because I can't afford any help, so it won't affect me. But it's only a matter of time before the agricultural workers union is up in arms about the way wages are being cut and men getting sacked. I can see a strike coming on, and that'll do none of us any good. I think we've got to do something about it before it all gets out of hand."

The leadership qualities that had taken George Grundy through the army ranks from private to sergeant major in less than three years were beginning to show. Just as he had done when they were in the Borsetshires together, Daniel fell in behind him.

"You're obviously right about problems, George, but what do you think we can do? Don't we all have to try to sort things out for ourselves?"

"I don't see how we can do anything ourselves. It's the government that's got us into this mess and it's that lot at Whitehall that'll have to get us out of it."

Bill Sawyer spluttered in his beer.

"You don't honestly think politicians care about farmers, do you? You don't think it was for our benefit that they introduced the Corn Laws in the middle of the war? It wasn't us that they were worrying about when they decided to guarantee our prices. They were just trying to save their own skins because the war was going wrong for them and the Jerry U-boats were sinking so many of our ships that there would have been a massive food shortage if they hadn't done something. It didn't take them very long after the war to lose sympathy with us, did it? They didn't think they needed us any more so they just went back to all their bloody, high falutin, free-trade ideas. That's what's made Britain nothing more than a dumping ground for all the cheap food in the world. How are farmers supposed to compete with that?"

George Grundy was delighted with this unexpected support from the usually reticent and very conservative farmer.

"You're dead right about that, Bill. All they ever care about is their own skins, and what we've got to do is to get together and raise enough stink for them to think we can cause them a lot of bother."

In this discussion Daniel heard the echoes of a conversation he'd had with George Lawson-Hope only a week or so earlier. The young squire had been complaining bitterly about the government and the heavy taxes they had imposed. He had said he was thinking of trying to persuade the country landowners to get together to lobby Parliament.

"Maybe we ought to talk to the squire? He's got problems, too, and it might be useful for us all to get together."

"Come off it, Daniel. The landed gentry don't have the same sort of problems as we have, and even if they did they'd hardly be likely to want to discuss it with a crowd of tenant farmers like us. Now would they?"

"Maybe you're right, George, but there's nothing to be lost by talking to George Lawson-Hope. He's not like the old squire at all, and when I saw him last week he was spitting as much blood about the politicians as you are now."

"Why was that?"

"Something to do with the new death duties he has to pay because he inherited his father's estate. He says he's got to pay out something around forty per cent of the estate's value to the taxman."

"I must admit that doesn't seem right . . . not when you remember that the old man did his bit in the army during the war. No, the lad's right, Daniel. Forty per cent is bloody savage."

George Grundy was proving that wartime camaraderie had a lasting quality. He might not have many complimentary things to say for the landed gentry, but his old colonel was different. Daniel noticed the slight softening of his attitude.

"Aye, and the only way young George can raise the money to pay the taxman is by selling off some land. He offered to sell me Brookfield, but I couldn't even begin to think about buying it. I couldn't afford to, and with the collapse of grain prices, my guess would be that very few other tenants will be able to buy. That means the landlords have got as much trouble on their plates as we have."

There was a pause in the conversation while Bill Sawyer ordered another round of drinks.

"Damn the landlords!"

Percy Hood had said very little since his dominoes game had been abandoned, but he had clearly been thinking hard.

"You ought not to have any truck with them. Of course they have problems, and that's the very reason you should be keeping away from them. If they're going to solve anybody's problems, it'll be their own! If the squire has to pay out as much as forty per cent in death duties, it's because his land is worth more than £2 million. I read the papers, you know, and that's what it said in the *Daily Mail*. I wouldn't mind paying tax on £2 million, would you? I wish your brother Ben was here, Daniel. He'd soon convince you that you and the gentry are on different sides and always will be. They might seem quite sympathetic when you've got minor problems and they can throw a few crumbs in your direction without it costing them much, but when the chips are down it's always a different story. No amount of forelock tugging will do you any good then."

Daniel remembered the many times his brother had argued that socialism was the only answer to the country's problems. He wondered how pleased he would have been by the results of the General Election in Britain only two days earlier. The Conservatives had been re-elected with another big majority, but the Labour Party had done very well, replacing the Liberals as the main opposition party for the first time.

"What do you suggest, Percy? That we all join the Labour Party and ask Ramsay MacDonald to solve our problems for us?"

Silas Winter gave a snort.

"That'll do us no good at all. The politicians aren't interested in farming folk. They don't care what happens to us any more. They're only concerned about the big towns and cities now. The Tories and the Liberals think that's where all the money is, and the Labour Party are much more interested in what's going on in the factories and industrial centres because that's where all the unions are and that's where they'll get the biggest part of their vote. It's the bloody industrial revolution that's sealed our fate. There's no way of turning that back!"

Percy Hood wasn't quite sure whether or not to continue with the argument. Because he was only a baker, he often felt a bit of an outsider in conversations about farming. He didn't want his friends to think he was trying to tell them how to run their affairs, but he decided to take the chance.

"Look, as I see it the Tories and the Liberals are on the way down. The Labour Party nearly doubled its vote, and they've got twice as many Members of Parliament as they had in 1918. But if they're going to stand any chance of winning next time round, they're going to have to look for votes from people like you. The time when they're looking for votes is the only time they're likely to listen to you. Look at what's happened in New Zealand. The politicians needed the farmers' votes so much they've more or less turned their policies upside down. They even call the Reform Party the Farmers' Party, now. That's what you ought to be after."

On both occasions that Daniel Archer had voted – in the 1918 General Election and in the one just gone – he'd cast his vote for the Tory party. He'd never told anyone else how he'd voted because he considered it his own affair, but he felt the need to justify his decision now, even if only to himself.

"I don't think you can blame the Conservative government as easily as that. None of us complained when they asked us to increase the acreage under crops, and none of us complained when they decided to guarantee prices. We did an awful lot better during the war years than most of the poor folk living in the towns did. I bet none of you ever felt guilty about that, did you? When the war ended and they still agreed to go on with the price guarantees, did any of us complain then? We couldn't expect that to last forever."

Percy Hood shook his head sadly.

"Honestly, Daniel, you sound as if you think earning your living from the land is a privilege."

"Aye, well sometimes I think it is. I certainly wouldn't want to have to live in a big town and have to clock in and out of work at a factory every day."

Percy was almost speechless.

"Don't be daft, lad. It isn't a privilege. You've got a right to earn a living for yourself and your family. You shouldn't feel beholden to the government or the squire or any other god-like figure."

Percy would have gone on at greater length, but George Grundy interrupted him.

"We're getting away from the point. I was talking about the financial problems that we're all going to face sooner or later, and none of you seems to be bothered about that. Here we are on the night before what we know is going to be one of the poorest harvest festivals there's ever been in Ambridge, and none of us has the gumption to see what we can do about it."

Worried that there was more talking than drinking going on, Jake Burton came into the snug and asked in a voice heavy with sarcasm whether they had worked out whose turn it was to buy the next round of drinks.

"This here place happens to be a pub, you know, not a political debating shop. Why don't you arrange a meeting of the NFU and thrash it out there?"

The National Farmers Union, set up fourteen or fifteen years earlier, had become an important organisation but not many Ambridge farmers bothered to attend the meetings locally because they were always held in Borchester. In fact, George Grundy was the only one of those present who had ever been to one.

"That's not a bad idea, Jake. How about it, Daniel? Shall you and I get the county secretary to fix something up?"

Just as Daniel was agreeing to this, the door of the snug opened and Walter Gabriel came in.

"Hello, me old pals, me old beauties!"

With his corncrake voice and his strong Borsetshire accent, Walter always managed to give the impression of being years older than he was. Daniel had to remind himself that Walter was actually a couple of months younger than him.

"You're late tonight, Walter."

"I've been listening to the wireless!"

There was great pride in his voice because he knew quite well that none of his friends had so far heard any broadcasts from the new British Broadcasting Company. The service had started a few days earlier; so far only a few people had bought the required licences.

"You haven't bought a wireless, have you?"

"Where did you hear it?"

"What was it like?"

"Was it a concert?"

"Did you hear the news on it?"

Walter, who loved nothing more than to be the centre of attention, was delighted with the response.

"Of course I haven't bought a wireless. I heard it at the vicarage. The vicar's got a lovely big set with three valves so that he can hear everything broadcast from the London station as well as what comes out from Birmingham."

"Tell us what you heard, Walter."

"First of all I heard a woman singing. I don't know what her song was, but she sounded lovely. The vicar said she was a soprano. Her voice was ever so clear; she could have been in the room with you."

"Is that all?"

George Grundy sounded disappointed.

"No. I heard a man speaking about the news as well."

"What news? What's happened?"

Daniel feared that there might have been another unexplained death or something.

"What do you mean, what happened? I just told you. I heard the man speaking the news."

"Yes, but what was the news he was speaking about, Walter?"

"I don't know, Daniel. I was so excited that I didn't really hear what he was saying."

Everyone laughed and Daniel was relieved.

"When did the vicar get his wireless, Walter?"

"Well, that's the point, you see. He only got it today and he asked me if I would help the man who brought it to put it in and make it work."

Daniel could hardly control his laughter.

"But, Walter, you don't know anything about the wireless. How could you help?"

Walter sounded hurt.

"I'm very good at figuring things out as you well know, Daniel Archer. Who was it that came to your rescue when you needed a bit of clever work with your horse's harness? How many times have you been grateful for my help in turning out things you can't get from the blacksmith?"

"Yes, I know you're very clever, Walter, but fixing up a wireless is a job for an expert, isn't it?"

"Well . . . yes . . . it is, I suppose . . . but this other man was the expert. I was just there to help."

"So what did you have to do?"

"I had to open and shut the door."

"Open and shut the door? What on earth for?"

"Because that's part of the aerial, of course."

There was now a universal mixture of mirth and bewilderment on all five faces in the snug. Daniel wasn't sure whether Walter was being Walter or if he were telling the truth.

"How can a door be part of a wireless aerial, Walter?"

"Well, you see, without an aerial you wouldn't be able to hear anything unless you were very close to the station the programme was being broadcast from. That's what the man told me. The aerial is really just a long piece of wire that comes out of the back of the set, but it's what you do with it that's important."

The temptation to tease Walter was too much for Silas Winter.

"If it's called a wireless, why do you have to have a wire coming out of the back?"

"Don't interrupt him, for heaven's sake, Silas. We'll be here all night, otherwise!"

"If you really want to know about it all, you should listen to me properly and stop making fun of me."

"Sorry, Walter. We're all ears!"

"This aerial thing . . . it's a long piece of wire that comes out of the back of the wireless, and because it's so long you have to wind it around something. The man told the vicar that he could wind it around a kind of frame that he could then pretend was a firescreen or something, but the vicar didn't like the look of it."

"What about the door?"

"I'm getting to that. An alternative is to attach the wire to a pole out in the back garden, but the vicar didn't like that idea very much either because it would have meant boring a hole in the door or window frame. That's when the man suggested the door."

"Wouldn't you get electrocuted if the wire is on the door handle?"

"You don't put it on the handle. You tack it around the edge of the door and then you open the door to point it in the direction of the station you want to hear."

"Isn't it very cold if you have to leave the door open?"

"It isn't the outside door you use!"

"And was that all there was to it, Walter?"

"It wasn't easy. While the man twiddled the knobs on the wireless, I kept having to hold the door open at every angle. It was only because I did that so well that we eventually got the right sound. The vicar was ever so pleased. He said I could go there and hear the wireless again if I wanted to."

Daniel had read in the papers that the Post Office had printed around two million licences ready for a great demand. However, fewer than twenty thousand people had bothered to apply for one. After hearing

145

Walter's explanation about the aerial, he wasn't in the least bit surprised. There couldn't be many people around daft enough to open and close doors every time they wanted to hear anything. The wireless looked like being another nine-day wonder.

CHAPTER FOURTEEN

Undoing the stud that held the stiff, white collar tightly around his neck, Daniel Archer gave a sigh of relief. Throughout the funeral service the collar had threatened to strangle him like some medieval instrument of torture. It may have had something to do with the lump that came into his throat as the vicar gave thanks for what he called Phoebe Archer's life of diligent toil.

Now back at home in the privacy of his bedroom, with all the mourners gone and Doris busy in the kitchen, Daniel had more time to think about his mother and to be more honest in his assessment of her life, a life that had been cut short at the early age of forty-seven by a heart attack.

In the church the vicar had talked about her loyalty to her family and her commitment to the land, as befitted the wife and mother of farmers. At the graveside everyone had been concerned to say what a wonderful worker she had been in the Women's Institute, on the organising committee of the village fete, and on the various church groups of which she had been a member.

No one had said she had enjoyed her life, and that was what was causing Daniel to reflect as he gazed out on the daisy-covered pastures beyond the cobbled yard. He couldn't put his hand on his heart and say his mother had had a happy life. Certainly, there had been good times, and he would always remember the picnics on Lakey Hill when his father was alive and the whole family would spend Sunday afternoons up there. He'd remember Christmastimes, the harvest festivals and lots of other special occasions when his mother's warm smile and infectious laughter added to everyone's enjoyment.

There were other things to remember, however.

Like most of the country girls of her generation, she'd had to go into service when she was thirteen.

147

Unlike Doris, she had landed in an unhappy household where the servants were treated like slaves. Phoebe had sometimes told stories of having to get out of bed at four in the morning to start on the dirtiest chores so that she could be cleaned up before the housekeeper arrived to inspect her hands and fingernails at six. She also spoke of the young daughter of the same Victorian family who was forced to get up at seven to practise the piano in the coldest room in the house because it was the one farthest from where her parents slept. They weren't prepared to sacrifice their sleep for the benefit of their daughter's musical education. The little mite was only three. His mother had sometimes cried when she recalled her ordeal.

Daniel remembered, too, the sadness he had seen in his mother's eyes when he had gone off to join the army. She hadn't said anything and neither had he, but he knew they had both been afraid that he wouldn't come back. He guessed that she must have felt the same agony when Ben enlisted, and then when young Frank took off for New Zealand. He hadn't been there on either occasion, but he was there, of course, when Ben had suddenly upped and left on that fateful Boxing Day in 1918. Again his mother hadn't said much, but he knew that was because she never liked showing her emotions in public . . . a hangover from her own childhood when children were expected neither to be seen nor heard, except when it suited their parents.

More recently Phoebe had been very upset by the death of Jesse Plant. He had killed himself because, like so many other farmers, he had fallen on hard times and couldn't see a way out of his problems. All his workers had been laid off, and Mrs Plant and her family had gone to live somewhere near Borchester. Wimberton Farm was now lying derelict. The house was unpainted and the hedges around the fields were uncut. It was a stark reminder that life was not easy in an uncompromising countryside. Ambridge had been lucky that Jesse Plant was the only local farmer to have got into serious trouble, but there were plenty of other cases around the county, and all of them seemed to touch his mother.

Perhaps, however, the worst memory of all was of the day he had come back from France. That was a full month after his father had died, and he had expected his mother to be more or less back to normal by then. She wasn't. He had never seen such deep-rooted grief. He wouldn't have recognised her if she hadn't been sitting in her favourite chair in the kitchen at Brookfield. She looked drawn and haggard. There were deep, black rings around her eyes, and the eyes themselves were lifeless. She hadn't even risen to greet him. It had taken her a long time to get used to being a widow . . . if she ever did.

Yes, Daniel thought, there were all too many sadnesses in her life.

"Are you all right, Daniel?"

He hadn't heard Doris coming up the stairs.

"Aye, I'm all right, love. I was just doing a bit of thinking."

"About your mother?"

"Aye."

Doris slipped her hand into his and squeezed it.

"Would you like to be on your own for a while?"

"No, lass. I could do with your company to shake me out of myself. I've been getting a bit maudlin."

"There's nothing wrong with that at a time like this. Why not come downstairs and we'll have a chat over a cup of tea?"

"That will be nice, Doris. You and I haven't had much time to do that since we got wed."

Downstairs, Doris poured the strong tea into Daniel's mug and added the heaps of sugar he liked so much.

"Did you want to talk about your mother?"

"Do you mind?"

"No, of course not!"

"I was just thinking about her and I suddenly realised that I didn't really know whether or not you could say she'd had a happy life."

"Oh, Daniel, of course she was happy. My mother always said she was one of the happiest souls in the village. Whatever do you mean?"

"Well, I didn't mean that she wasn't happy by nature, but I just wonder how life had treated her. Could you say that overall she'd had a happy life?"

"That's a very deep question and I don't know as how you'll ever get an answer to it. The only person who could have given you an answer was your mother herself."

"I feel very guilty that I never knew enough of how she felt about things. Our Ben once told me that as well. He said I was too self-centred and never worried about other people. He was right. I hardly ever asked my mother about her worries or problems."

Doris leaned across the table and held his hand again.

"What exactly is it that's bothering you, Daniel?"

"I don't know. I just feel that maybe if I'd taken the time and the trouble to understand her more, I'd have been able to do more for her. It was always her who seemed to be doing things for me. She was terrific about the farm, you know. There wasn't a job she wouldn't tackle as well as any man. I don't think I ever bothered to tell her how grateful I was."

"Don't you worry on that score, Daniel. Your mother knew how much you appreciated her. You didn't have to say anything. Don't forget she was a farmer's wife, and farmers' wives never expect any show of gratitude for the work they do. They get used to being taken for granted, too."

Daniel looked at her guiltily.

"Oh, heck, Doris, have I been taking you for granted?"

Doris laughed and gave his hand another squeeze.

"Don't you worry about me, lad. I know my place around Brookfield, and I'm more than happy with my lot!"

"Are you really happy?"

"Of course I am. I've told you before that all I ever wanted to be was a farmer's wife . . . that's after I gave up the idea of becoming a famous singer!"

"Don't you miss the grand life at the Manor House?"

"I was never part of that life, Daniel. Mrs Lawson-Hope is a very generous lady, but even she didn't exactly encourage her lady's maid to join in the social events of the house!"

"What was it like being a servant? That's one of the questions I always wanted to ask my mother."

"I suppose it was something like you being in the army. You were always being told what to do and when to do it. The thing that upset me most was the way the other servants used to line up in a kind of pecking order and act as if they were as grand as the people they worked for."

"I was thinking more about dignity and things like that. I mean, did you mind having to bow and scrape to people?"

"You never think about it. Don't forget, I went into service when I was thirteen, so I never knew anything different. I just thought it was polite to curtsy and call people 'sir' or 'madam' or whatever. Your mother and I talked about that. It didn't bother her either."

"Did you and her have much chance to get to know each other in the few months since you came to Brookfield?"

Doris laughed. Her dark curls bobbed as she threw her head back.

"You don't think two women could share a kitchen for even five minutes and not get to know each other, do you? Yes, we had lots of time to talk to each other. I think she missed not having a daughter of her own, and she loved to gossip – while we were working, in case you think we sat around chatting!"

"I didn't know she would have liked a daughter!"

"Well, she'd hardly mention that to three great hulking brutes, who no doubt each imagined themselves to be the apple of her eye. Anyway, it didn't stop her being very proud of you and your brothers."

"Did she ever say anything about Ben and Frank?"

"Funny thing, that. She talked quite a lot about Frank and how he was doing so well out in New Zealand, but she never once mentioned Ben. Whenever *I* did, she usually managed to change the subject. What is it about Ben? You don't say much about him, either. Is he the black sheep of the family or something?"

"No, it's not that, Doris. It's a long story."

"Well, I'm not in any great hurry to get on with the clearing up."

More than fifty friends and relatives had come back to Brookfield after the funeral, and the tea cups and other dishes were stacked in the sink waiting to be washed up.

"I'll tell you what, Doris. I'll do the drying and we can talk about it while we're getting things out of the way."

To the clatter of the washing up and the occasional exclamation from Doris, Daniel recounted the story of the Christmas party at her house and then the terrible fight in the barn, followed by Ben's sudden departure.

"Poor Ben. He must have been very mixed up just to disappear in the middle of the night like that. Would you have gone if it had been the other way around?"

"I don't know, Doris. I don't think I could have done. I would have been too frightened of the unknown. I would never have dreamed of going to Canada. I don't have Ben's sense of adventure. I'm really a bit of a stick-in-the-mud, as you know."

Doris smiled cheekily.

"I *do* know. How long did it take you to finally propose to me?"

"Aye, well, that was a bit to do with our Ben as well."

"How do you mean?"

"Well, in the middle of the fight he accused me of digging myself into Brookfield while he was digging trenches in Flanders. Then he suggested that I'd taken the chance to court you while he was fighting the war. I felt awful about it, and really that's why I was never able to come to see you for ages after that. If I'd proposed and you'd accepted, it would have looked as if Ben had been right. Do you understand, Doris?"

152

"Yes, I understand. You're a sensitive soul, right enough. You're just like your mother. She was very sensitive to other people's feelings."

"Do you know what I'd like to do now, love? I'd like to go back down to the churchyard without all the crowd and just say goodbye to her properly. Would you mind? I'd like you to come with me."

"Oh Daniel, that's a lovely idea. Of course I'll come with you."

They both went upstairs, where Doris put on her best coat and Daniel forced himself back into the stiff collar and put on his dark jacket.

As they walked past the big meadow Daniel looked at the daisies that appeared to be growing almost as you watched them.

"I think we may put the cows back out to pasture tomorrow."

Doris nodded her assent. Walter Gabriel had told her about some story about how to tell when the cattle should be put back into the fields after the winter but, Walter being Walter, she didn't know the truth of it and didn't want to show her ignorance. She was determined to learn everything there was to know about being a farmer's wife – Daniel's mother had been very helpful about passing on as many tips as she could over their shared chores, but she'd never got round to the art of grazing. Daniel must have been reading Doris's mind.

"Has Walter ever told you his old wives' tale about how you know when to put the cattle out?"

"Yes, but I can't remember it very well. He's got so many tales that I keep getting them all mixed up. Do you mean the one about being able to stand on five daisies?"

"That's the one. He says his granny always reckoned that the time to put the cows out was when you could cover five daisies with one foot."

"I never know whether or not to believe Walter and his granny."

"Well, I wouldn't like to think what would happen to Brookfield if we relied on their advice, but the bit about

153

the daisies isn't all that far-fetched. The daisies don't come out until the soil temperature has risen after all the ground frosts – and that's what you need for good grass, too. Anyway, we'll soon see if tomorrow's right."

"How will you know?"

"The cows'll tell us themselves."

Doris wasn't sure if Daniel was teasing her.

"How do you mean?"

"You can help me tomorrow and you can see for yourself. If the pasture is to their liking, they'll go trotting around the field kicking their legs in the air."

"What about the milking now? Will I have to do that out in the fields?"

Daniel couldn't help laughing.

"I'm sorry, love. I keep forgetting that you're new to living on a farm. No, we won't send you out with your yoke and buckets and a milking stool to catch yourself a few gallons. We bring the cows in for milking just as you've been doing it throughout the winter."

"Well, that's a relief!"

Daniel laughed again and gave her a hug.

"Come on, lass, that's farming school over for the day. Let's get on down to the churchyard."

Hand in hand, they walked down the lane, enjoying the spring sunshine and the bluebells growing among the hedgerows. Daniel's earlier sadness had gone. Instead, he reflected on how much his mother must have enjoyed her few short months as mentor and teacher to his new bride.

As they walked through the village Percy Hood came out of his shop to offer his condolences and to apologise for not being able to attend the funeral. While they were chatting, Nancy Sawyer came out of her shop to offer her sympathy, too, but she very quickly moved the conversation on to other topics, ranging from the spring weather to Doris's spring coat. Nancy was one of life's enthusiasts, and she would never allow a little thing like death to dampen her spirits. Perhaps it was because her shop was only a stone's throw from the churchyard that she was able to take death so much for granted. From her front step she had been able to witness every burial that had ever taken place in Ambridge for the past twenty years and more.

It was probably an ancestor of Nancy's that had a hand in siting the churchyard in the heart of the village, so that the dead were separated from the quick only by some Victorian iron railings that ran alongside the main street between the houses and the church.

In fact, the verger often complained that the railings were not effective enough in keeping out the living – the local children were never slow to chase their balls or other paraphernalia of play into the graveyard, and they had been known to cause the odd bit of damage from time to time – nothing very serious, just enough to irritate the verger.

On their way between the village stores and the entrance to the little churchyard, Daniel and Doris were stopped five or six times more by sympathetic neighbours. Daniel was surprised to receive so much attention.

"Folk are very kind, aren't they? It's very good of them to take the trouble to talk to us. I didn't know so many of them even knew us."

"Honestly, Daniel, sometimes I think you must have been living with a paper bag over your head. Everyone in Ambridge knows you!"

"I don't know how, Doris. I hardly ever get beyond The Bull when I come to the village and I only see the same crowd of men there most times."

"Well, your reputation obviously precedes you. Even when I was working for Mrs Lawson-Hope I knew that you were doing a grand job in developing Brookfield into one of the best farms in the district. Even the squire said so and people do talk to each other, you know. They're not like you. Sometimes I get the feeling that you think words are meant to be kept for special occasions!"

Daniel had to weigh up whether he was being criticised or teased. He decided he was being teased.

"That's judged by your standards, Doris. But then you could talk the hind leg off a donkey."

They were both laughing as they pushed open the squeaky gate that led into the churchyard but as they walked along the footpath to the new grave they lapsed into silence. Dan looked down on the simple headstone that had been put there when his father died.

In Loving Memory of

JOHN ARCHER

devoted husband to Phoebe

and beloved father of

Daniel, John Benjamin and Frank

Gone to His Rest

October 7th., 1917

Beneath that, Daniel had arranged for a new inscription to be added.

PHOEBE ARCHER

United with her husband
in everlasting peace

April 20th., 1923

"Do you think the inscription is all right, Doris? I didn't know what to put. I wanted it to be very plain because I thought she would prefer that."

Daniel spoke almost in a whisper. Doris could see that he was close to tears.

"It's exactly right, Daniel."

For ten minutes they stood in total silence, Daniel with his head bowed and Doris holding his hand.

"Thank you for coming with me, Doris."

Daniel took out his handkerchief and blew his nose.

"I feel much better now. I don't know what it is about funerals, but I just didn't feel right with so many people around. She and I spent a lot of time together . . . just the two of us, because Dad had died and Ben and Frank had gone off abroad."

"It's a shame that neither of your brothers could get back in time for the funeral."

"I don't think Mother would have minded them not being here. She always desperately wanted them to come back to Ambridge, but she accepted that they wouldn't. I think she understood why not. She was never a possessive mother."

"Do you think we'll ever see Ben or Frank again?"

"I think they would both like to come home, at least for a visit, but whether or not they'll ever be able to afford it is a different question."

"Maybe when this depression is over and we make our fortune out of Brookfield, we can send them the price of the tickets as a present? Wouldn't that be nice, Daniel?"

Daniel smiled at his wife. She had a heart of gold, and he could hardly believe his luck that they had finally married after such a long time. He gave her another hug.

"What would you like to do now, Doris? Do you want to go for a walk up Lakey Hill or would you rather go straight back to Brookfield?"

"I'd like to go home, if you don't mind. I'm feeling a bit tired and there are still quite a few things to be done around the house."

"Don't worry about that. You can do that in the morning."

"No, Daniel, I can't do it in the morning. I've got to go to the doctor . . . I think I'm going to have a baby!"

BORCHESTER ECHOES

Phil and Jill Archer's younger daughter Elizabeth, is using her job in the tele-sales department of the *Borchester Echo* to try and break through into the world of journalism. Always on the lookout for news stories to impress proprietor Jack Woolley, she enlists the help of her boyfriend Robin Fairbrother and of winebar-owner Nelson Gabriel to investigate what she imagines to be a swindle being conducted by a local antiques dealer.

Meanwhile her private life is carried on at a hectic pace. Robin Fairbrother offers her the entrée to the world of fast cars and good living, but she is still amused by the antics of hooray-Henry Nigel Pargetter, and cannot resist a minor fling with Terry Barford, serving with the Army in Germany, who she joins for a weekend in Berlin.

Elizabeth gets her story . . . but not quite the job on the *Borchester Echo* she anticipated.

RETURN TO AMBRIDGE

Jack Archer, son of Dan and Doris, did not have a distinguished war service – he barely stepped outside the regimental stores. Demobbed in 1944, and still only 21, he returns to Ambridge demoralised and dispirited, engulfed by the grey drabness of post-war Britain.

Married to Peggy, a young London girl formerly in the ATS, he finds it difficult to settle down to the responsibilities of family life. He feels overshadowed by his father, and by his younger brother Philip, already clearly marked out as Dan's eventual successor at Brookfield Farm. It is only Peggy's cheerful and resilient cockney spirit, rising to the challenge of a new life in the heart of the English countryside, that keeps alive their efforts to run their smallholding and bring up a young family. For her, the Borsetshire village is a little corner of paradise, but for Jack, in his return to Ambridge lie the seeds of his eventual breakdown and retreat into alcoholism.